lust

lust

bisexual

erotica

by

marilyn

jaye

lewis

a alyson books

los angeles

MANUFACTURED IN THE UNITED STATES OF AMERICA.

THIS TRADE PAPERBACK ORIGINAL IS PUBLISHED BY ALYSON PUBLICATIONS,
P.O. BOX 4371, LOS ANGELES, CALIFORNIA 90078-4371.
DISTRIBUTION IN THE UNITED KINGDOM BY TURNAROUND PUBLISHER SERVICES LTD.,
UNIT 3, OLYMPIA TRADING ESTATE, COBURG ROAD, WOOD GREEN,
LONDON N22 6TZ ENGLAND.

FIRST EDITION: OCTOBER 2004

04 05 06 07 08 a 10 9 8 7 6 5 4 3 2 1

ISBN 1-55583-816-2

LIBRARY OF CONGRESS CATALOGING-IN-PUBLICATION DATA
LEWIS, MARILYN JAYE.
  LUST : BISEXUAL EROTICA / BY MARILYN JAYE LEWIS.—1ST ED.
  ISBN 1-55583-816-2
  1. BISEXUALITY—FICTION. 2. EROTIC STORIES, AMERICAN. 3. BISEXUAL WOMEN—
FICTION. I. TITLE.
PS3612.E9968L87 2004
813'.6—DC22   2004052927

CREDITS
COVER PHOTOGRAPHY BY ALAIN DAUSSIN/PHOTOGRAPHER'S CHOICE COLLECTION.
COVER DESIGN BY MATT SAMS.

Dedicated in loving memory to Paul Martin,
1959–1999
My first believer—I never forget

contents

three for the money

Yesterday I went to a funeral uptown. In the morning when I left my apartment, it had been the proverbial spring day, birds chirping, daffodils blooming in the park—the works. But by the time I came up from the subway station an hour and a half later, it had begun to rain. Funerals are a bit like rain dances in that way; something about people gathered together in mourning, and the sky itself cries.

The dead guy, Marten Santos, had been notoriously rich and depraved. He had never tried to pass as righteous, though, never pretended to be perfect. We all knew about his peculiar tastes and erratic passions, and we loved him for them. Nevertheless, he'd been raised a strict Roman Catholic, and so the funeral was a stuffy, conservative affair, held at Our Lady of Divine Sorrows. After the funeral, as the teary-eyed pallbearers removed the casket from the church and solemnly loaded it into the back of the hearse, Our Lady's bell tolled mournfully, sounding all the more poignant in the gray drizzle of rain. He was a man who was going to be missed by a lot of good people.

Mr. Santos had been one of my favorite tricks. When he died suddenly of a heart attack three days ago, the newspaper said that he was pushing seventy. The year when he'd been one of my regulars, he claimed to be fifty-five. It says a lot that after all these years I felt a sense of loss strong enough to compel me to attend his funeral. But then, he hadn't always been a trick. With Mr. Santos, I'd done the unthinkable and allowed a favorite john to become a lover, or nearly so. The shame of that slip-up on my part and a difficult scene he put me through in a cheap hotel room had caused us to go our separate ways but had made me no less fond of him.

I don't turn tricks anymore, I haven't for years. I'm almost forty now, and I work in a respectable office and earn a respectable living. I present a very hard-assed, successful-bitch version of myself to the world, which has helped me to succeed and keep my past where it should be: in the past. The frantic, frenetic survival skills acquired by all New Yorkers make the town a forgiving place. As long as you don't wind up at the heart of a sordid public scandal in a court of law—where New Yorkers show their ugly side and revel in seeing your past mistakes slung at you like so much mud—you can do just about anything to get ahead in this town and not have to worry too much that it'll come back to haunt you.

Mr. Santos and I first met in an upscale espresso shop on the upper east side. This was back in the '80s, when a whole lot of people had money to burn. Mr. Santos was friends with the owner, Hajid, who was one of my regulars too. Hajid liked getting blow jobs behind the desk in his office, which was in the basement of the coffeehouse. It was decidedly downscale in that dark, damp, vermin-infested cellar. However, a simple blow job, as long as I was willing to have my pants around my knees and keep my naked ass out for his viewing pleasure, lasted only about ten minutes and garnered me 200 tax-free dollars, so I found ways to make even that location seem erotic.

The evening I met Mr. Santos, I was actually just having coffee. Hajid and I were on friendly terms. He introduced me to Mr. Santos with a nod and a wink, and Mr. Santos pulled up a chair. He got right down to the business of getting to know me better. He ended the meeting by paying my modest tab and then asking me for my phone number, which, of course, I gave him, since it was obvious he was loaded—even more so than Hajid.

Our trysts started out simple and straightforward. Mr. Santos would always arrange for me to meet him in other rich people's high-class apartments. The people he knew went on extended vacations, traveled on business to faraway places, or had primary homes in other countries. Mr. Santos was married back then, and apparently he and his other married male friends formed a cozy circle of infidels, each leaving the rest of the crew a key to their empty apartments for extramarital liaisons in their absence. I don't think the wives ever had a clue what was taking place in the sanctity of their homes while they were off on holiday.

I was never to touch anything, never allowed to get too comfortable in the jaw-dropping luxury of our trysting places. Mr. Santos liked anal, and that was pretty much the sole basis of our get-togethers at first. Without fanfare, he would unzip his trousers and let them fall unceremoniously to his ankles, along with his boxers. He'd slip on a rubber and slather it with the lube that he carried in his pocket in handy individual foil packets. Then I'd bend over anything steady and he'd slide his cock up my ass.

He fucked me like a man who had important meetings to get to—he usually came pretty quickly. I didn't have to say anything weird or dress in anything unusual. I simply had to show up with an absolutely clean asshole, bend over, and let him ream me; that was all he required. For that, I got $500 cash: five crisp $100 bills, folded in the middle, which he'd place under my nose while I was still bending over. Before he even pulled his cock out of me, I got paid.

There was something about the way he paid me that tended to make me feel a little humiliated, but he didn't seem to think twice about it. By the time I'd turn around, he'd have the used condom off and his trousers pulled up, and he'd be heading to the toilet to flush the condom down. He never said anything like, "Here's your money, you whore," or "Take that, bitch." He just had a funny habit of leaving it parked under my nose while my ass was still stuffed with him.

I remember when we had our first post-anal conversation. It was a day when he seemed to be at leisure, not pressed for time. On that day, he had wandered around the spacious apartment we were using, looking for the perfect place to bend me over. Making small talk, making jokes. "Bend over that chair there, let me see the view. Pull up your skirt. No, we can find something better."

When he finally decided on the perfect spot—an ergonomically correct artist's stool—he lifted my skirt himself, pulled my panties down (an intimate move he'd never made before), and then said, "You know what this reminds me of?"

My naked ass in the air, my thighs spread in anticipation, my head hanging down, I said, "No, what?"

"Church. This reminds me of church."

He didn't elaborate, and I had no idea what he was talking about. But the thought of church seemed to make him feel even more jovial. He sank to his knees and rimmed me, his hot, wet tongue expertly stroking my puckered hole. It felt sensational. I actually moaned and felt like touching myself.

Having his nose in my ass seemed to arouse his passion, for that day he fucked my ass vigorously, nearly knocking me off the stool several times; the mounting pressure of his thickening hard-on sucking in and out of my ass made me cry out. When he came, he pulled his cock out a little aggressively, gave me a resounding smack on my upturned ass, and said, "Here you go. Thanks, kiddo." And the money was once again placed in front of my face—on this occasion, I'd been staring at a parquet floor.

His breezy pre-sex conversing, combined with his sudden rugged manner with me during sex, made me see Mr. Santos in a different light. He was a handsome man, I decided as I watched him zip up his trousers and go off in search of the toilet. I still had my panties around my knees when he came back in the room. I was lingering in my little swoon.

"What's with you?" he asked.

Snapping out of it and feeling embarrassed, I moved to pull up my panties.

"No, wait." He stopped me. "Not yet. You feel like making a little extra money today?"

I was caught off guard. He fished out his wallet and surveyed its contents. "Well, I have ten whole dollars." He found this amusing. "What do you feel like doing for $10?"

"What did you have in mind?"

"I want to try something and see if I can make you come."

I never, under any circumstances, came with a trick. But Mr. Santos intrigued me. "You think you can make me come for $10?"

"Ten bucks and a nice dinner. What do you say to that? My wife's out of town and I've got all the time in the world. I'll make it up to you next time about the money. You know I'm good for it."

I was feeling game. I liked Mr. Santos. I wasn't worried about the money.

He told me to step out of my panties completely, then to squat down on the parquet floor. He told me that under no circumstances should I touch myself; he wanted to do all the work. He lubed two of his fingers, squatted down next to me, held me around my shoulders to sort of brace me, and then he stuck the two lubed fingers up my ass. He wiggled them vigorously in there, pushing hard against my perineum, rubbing the wall of muscle with all his strength.

"Oh, God," I squealed in sheer ecstasy, clutching him tight, a stream of piss suddenly squirting out of me, forming a puddle on the nice wood floor.

"Go for it, baby. Let everything go. We can clean this up later. Bear down on me."

I did as he suggested, pushing my asshole down around his hardworking fingers, never dreaming that I could be launched into orgasm like a rocket without direct pressure applied to my clit. But it happened. My thighs shook as I squatted and bore down, more fluids gushing out of my open piss hole. My body was overwhelmed by waves of pleasure as his fingers rubbed more vigorously against the pressure of my now frantically contracting sphincter.

When I was through hyperventilating and convulsing like a

lunatic, Mr. Santos was still holding me, smiling. "Did you come?" he asked, very pleased with himself.

I didn't take the extra $10 that day, but I took him up on his offer to buy me dinner and that was the beginning of a new chapter in our "business relationship."

He continued to pay me whenever we got together, but we talked more, he took more time with me, and he felt challenged to give me orgasms in unexpected ways. Soon he was paying for rooms in five-star hotels, where we'd disappear for entire days together, relying on room service for sustenance. He introduced blindfolds, light bondage, and spanking to the list of things we were now doing with each other regularly in a lavish king-size bed.

"Do you ever eat pussy?" he asked me one afternoon. "I mean, do you ever get asked to do that when you're out on a call?"

I looked at him uneasily, not at all pleased that the world of my other tricks was even remotely entering into our time together.

"Do you even know *how* to eat pussy?"

"Of course I do."

"You get paid to do that?"

"Sometimes." I didn't feel much like discussing it.

"I'd like to see you eat pussy, you know that?"

You and every other trick on earth, I told myself. The last thing I wanted was to bring another girl into our scene, a girl who might prove to be more novel than me, a girl who might walk off with his number in her purse and then I would lose my favorite trick. Mr. Santos was now the man I fantasized about when I was home alone in bed. I didn't think he would leave his wife for me, or anything like that, but I naively considered us lovers. I'd begun to hate the fact that he still paid me.

"What's that face for?" he said. "You aren't into pussy?"

"Girls are all right."

"I was thinking more along the lines of a woman—not a girl."

He had piqued my interest. "You mean you have someone in mind?"

"To be honest, there's a woman I've been seeing off and on for years, since before I was married. Occasionally, we get together when our spouses are otherwise detained, and we have sex. I told her about you. How much fun you are. How amenable you can be."

And whose idea was it to make it a threesome, I wondered suspiciously, hers or his?

"She'll pay you the same amount I do, so you'll get double your usual fee. It wouldn't be a question of taking advantage. I would really like to see you eat her pussy. And I think she has an idea of a scene of her own. She's very willing to pay you," he repeated. "I don't think she's ever paid anyone to do a scene with her. Or to have *any* kind of sex with her, for that matter. She's just a regular married woman, but a good friend of mine."

She sounded harmless enough. But you'd think after my years of turning tricks, I would have known beyond a doubt that people who sound harmless can be your most difficult customers when it's all said and done.

Still, I agreed to do the three-way. We made an appointment for an afternoon the following week. For some reason, we were meeting in a tacky hotel in midtown—gone was the luxury of the king-size bed, the crisp white sheets, and room service. Everything about the hotel they'd chosen was dingy, seedy, and low-class.

Mr. Santos had asked me to bring along an outfit that would be suitable for a naughty little girl routine. Even though I'd never gone to Catholic school myself, I had a vintage Catholic schoolgirl uniform that fit me perfectly. I figured Mr. Santos would get off on the religion thing, so that's what I packed for my change of clothes.

I'd been getting steadily more into the idea of the three-way as the day had approached. Anything that involved the unpredictability of Mr. Santos's lusty libido aroused my own sexual appetites. He was nothing like my average trick. So when I knocked on the hotel room door that afternoon, I was already horny, already sopping wet between my legs. Until Mr. Santos let me into the room and introduced me to his woman friend.

Oh, my God, I realized in sick horror, *it's Mrs. Hamilton.*

She'd been my tenth-grade sociology teacher. A woman who'd made my life a living hell for an entire year. I was certain it was her. To this day, I don't know if she recognized me too. If she did, she never once let on. But I *knew* it was her. She was simply using a fake name, like a lot of tricks do.

"Call me either Daddy or Sir today," Mr. Santos was instructing me. "And this is your new stepmother, Louise."

Louise? They couldn't come up with anything less corny than Louise?

I had that feeling of panic in my gut that I used to get in my early days of hustling—I wanted to bolt. But then I focused on the money: $1,000 cash for a single afternoon's work. It would be worth it. But I saw immediately that it was going to be just that—work.

Mrs. Hamilton had never been an unattractive woman; it was just that she'd always been a mean bitch of a teacher. In my years since high school, she'd taken good care of herself and managed to stay attractive. I figured that if she knew Mr. Santos, she must have money too, and that always helps women stay good-looking. Yet it made me wonder why she'd chosen to teach at all. Perhaps for the sick thrill of tormenting teenagers?

"Louise wants to help you change clothes," Mr. Santos told me. "It'll give you two a chance to get comfortable with each other. I'm going to run across the street to the liquor store. This trashy hotel doesn't even supply booze."

Shit. He was leaving me alone with her. The dreaded moment was starting to look even worse. Not only would I have to get naked for Mrs. Hamilton, I would have to be completely alone with her while it happened. No horny Mr. Santos around to use as a buffer zone.

When he was gone, she went right into efficient teacher mode. "Come here," she said flatly. "Let's get you out of those clothes and into something more appropriate."

She didn't act at all nervous to be around a prostitute, to be doing a scene. I wondered if she was anybody's horny lesbo stepmother in real life. The implications of that thought creeped me out. I had to force myself to keep my mind a blank.

Mrs. Hamilton was going through my bag, pulling out my change of clothes. She seemed to recognize the uniform for what it was—something *real* girls wore in *real* high schools. "Are you Catholic?" she asked. "Not that it's any of my business."

"Yes," I said. "But I went to *public* schools." The sudden rudeness in my tone surprised even me.

She eyed me coolly, taking in that last remark. "Come over here," she said.

Shit. She was making me nervous. But I went over to her, and without hesitating she began to undress me. "Let me tell you something," she explained carefully, unbuttoning my shirt with manicured fingers. "While we're in the confines of this room, while we're on the clock, so to speak, I have no qualms whatsoever about making it very clear which one of us is on top." The sound of her words alone felt like a slap. She had my shirt off. She was moving to unfasten my bra; her fingers were touching the skin on my back, her face was close to mine. I didn't like it. "If you want to keep talking to me in that rude tone," she continued, "go right ahead. But consider yourself warned. I'm not afraid of girls like you. I deal with your kind every day."

My bra was off. My tits were right there in front of her, my nipples shivering to stiff points from the sudden change in temperature. How many times had I bared my tits for strange clients? But this took the cake for strangeness. I felt exposed.

She didn't touch me, though. She barely even paused to look at my nakedness. She was already on to my tight jeans, unzipping them, tugging them down to my ankles.

I was in that state of half-undressed nervousness when Mr. Santos came back to the room, carrying a fifth of gin and a large carton of orange juice.

Jesus, I wondered, how trashy are we going to get? Where was the top-shelf bourbon, or at the very least some cheap champagne?

"Well," he said, regarding us with satisfaction, "we're certainly progressing here. Anyone want a drink?"

We all did. Mr. Santos played bartender while keeping a keen eye on us.

Mrs. Hamilton had me completely undressed, except for my panties. Those she seemed to want to take more time with. She lowered them slowly, anticipating the unveiling of my neatly trimmed snatch. She was actually squatting down in front of me, apparently wanting an up-close-and-personal view. It made me even more uncomfortable—not so much that Mrs. Hamilton was squatting down in front of me, so obviously aroused by the imminent sight of another woman's pussy, but that I was getting off on it too. I was suddenly wet again.

"Good lord," she said quickly under her breath. She'd peeled my panties past my mound, rolled them partially down my thighs, and seen the strand of gooey wetness connecting my soaking hole to the cotton crotch of my underwear. She looked up at Mr. Santos, who was now standing next us, offers of drinks in his hand. "She's so wet," Mrs. Hamilton explained in quiet earnestness, as if the sight of a twat swollen in arousal pained her deliciously.

I took my drink from Mr. Santos and gulped it down. I needed fortification. Mrs. Hamilton was fucking *hot*. And now she was licking me, her mouth was actually on me down there, and I was getting off on it.

Jesus, I wondered; what was going to happen here? Alone, unsupervised, with two horny tricks who could get me this worked up; two people apparently intent on doing a pseudo-incest scene, with me playing the part of the helpless bottom; two tops wanting to have their way with me, and all of us downing cheap gin?

I was light-headed. I parted my legs as much as I could for Mrs. Hamilton, but it wasn't easy with my panties around my thighs. She held tight to my ass cheeks, her mouth flush with my mound. She moaned as her hot tongue slid eagerly around in the folds of my pussy lips, occasionally landing directly on the tip of my clit. I was soon so aroused by the lusty sounds she made that I actually held on to her head to keep myself steady. I had a handful of Mrs. Hamilton's hair in one hand and a plastic cup of gin and O.J. in the other. It all seemed so decadently tawdry. The cheap thrill of it made me press Mrs. Hamilton's face even closer to my snatch; I rubbed her face in the slippery folds of it. The horny bitch moaned even more.

Mr. Santos lit a cigarette. He stood close to us, watching it all unfold, feeling up my titties while he watched. Taking firm handfuls of titty flesh and squeezing, kneading, then tugging roughly on my stiff, aching nipples. He took a drag off his cigarette and then put his mouth on mine, forcing his exhaled smoke into my open mouth along with his tongue.

The feel of his tongue filling my mouth and Mrs. Hamilton's tongue deep between my sopping lips, while Mr. Santos kept up his avid mauling of my breasts—I thought I was going to come right on the spot.

But Mr. Santos had his thoughts elsewhere. He pulled away from me the second before I had a chance to come. "This is going to be good," he announced.

The sound of his voice seemed to bring Mrs. Hamilton back to earth. She got up from between my legs abruptly, her mouth a slick mess. She went straight for her drink, which was waiting for her on the dresser. I could see her mentally pulling herself together, reminding herself which one of us girls was on top.

Within moments, she was in stepmother mode. "I want you to go into the bathroom and put on your clothes. Your father and I want to be alone. We'll tell you when to come out."

I did as I was told, stopping first to refresh my drink. I closed myself up in the small, ugly bathroom and got into my uniform. Outside, I could hear the lusty sounds of them going at each other. Had they managed to strip out of their clothes in record time and begin fucking? Were they only partially undressed and sucking each other, or—just what were they doing? I was not only keenly curious, I was also jealous. I didn't want Mr. Santos to enjoy Mrs. Hamilton *that* much; after all, he was *my* lover.

Of course, I'd been instructed to stay put in the bathroom until I was given permission to come out. But that was all part of the scene. Naughty girls went wide-eyed into every opportunity to misbehave. Otherwise, you'd deprive your scene-mates of the chance to spank you bare-assed—or worse, depending on the infraction.

I quietly cracked open the bathroom door and peeked out at them.

I'll be damned, I thought.

They were fucking, all right. But they were, for the most part, still dressed. Mrs. Hamilton was bent over the foot of the bed, her pants tugged down to her knees, while Mr. Santos, cock out of his unzipped trousers, rode her hard from behind.

I was transfixed—they were in such a frenzy of lust. Plus the cheap booze had gone to my head. I couldn't believe I was watching Mrs. Hamilton get nailed, and in such an unflattering posture. Her white ass looked huge sticking out like that.

I worked my hand up under my skirt and inside my white panties. I wiggled my clit furiously as I watched them fuck like dogs.

As if on cue, Mrs. Hamilton glanced over at the bathroom door and caught me spying on them. It seemed to make her ass jut out even more, if that was possible. But she got a queer look on her face too, like she couldn't wait to get down and nasty on my own ass. I quickly closed the bathroom door and tried to mind my own business.

Naturally, it was too late; the incest-punishment scene was now in full swing. There was soon a knock on the bathroom door. When I opened it, it was "Daddy." He said, "Your stepmother wishes to speak to you."

I came out of the bathroom to find my "stepmother" stark naked, sitting on the bed. She looked good naked, but she looked angry. "Come over here," she said.

I expected to get thoroughly spanked by her, and I wasn't sure if I'd get off on it; she was still Mrs. Hamilton after all, a woman I had once despised. As I went to her, there was a fear in my belly reminiscent of what it had once felt like to face actual punishment as a child.

Daddy, still fully clothed, only his cock jutting out from his pants, sat down on the bed next to the naked "Louise." He had a stern expression on his face that made him look even more handsome. I was hoping he would force me to make it up to him somehow, but for now the emphasis was on Louise.

"Come closer," she said.

I stood directly in front of her, cowering in my schoolgirl uniform.

"What were you doing in there?" she demanded.

"Nothing."

"It was more than nothing, young lady. You were spying on us, weren't you?"

"Yes," I meekly confessed.

"Weren't you told to stay in there until someone came for you?"

"Yes."

"And why did you disobey me?"

"I don't know."

"I'll tell you why, because you're a dirty little girl, aren't you? What do you suppose happens to a dirty little girl who disobeys and sticks her nose where it doesn't belong?"

I gave it some serious thought. The look in Mrs. Hamilton's eye was dark and unpleasant. Mr. Santos, however, was in the throes of lust. He was watching it all while avidly stroking himself.

"I asked you a question," my stepmother went on. "What do you suppose happens to a dirty little girl who disobeys?"

"I don't know," I replied.

"I think you do."

I said nothing.

"Answer me."

"I guess I need to get spanked!" I finally blurted.

I was playing my part to the hilt now, and Mrs. Hamilton had succumbed completely to the erotic pull of her role. She was so obviously entranced by the power of her anger. "That's right. You need a good spanking to teach you a lesson. Get over here, right over my knee, young lady."

She grabbed me and pulled me over her knee, positioning me across her lap in such a way that everything between my legs was facing Mr. Santos. She lifted my skirt. "I'll teach you to be a dirty little girl," she said, lowering my panties with deliberate patience, slowly revealing the round, white globes of my ass, then tugging the panties down my thighs.

She held my wrists tight and then gave my ass a resounding spank. "Why do you dirty girls always have to learn how to behave the hardest way?" She gave me another well-placed, stinging spank.

"I want you to tell Daddy exactly what you did. Tell him why I'm so angry with you." Another severe smack heated my cheeks, making me jump.

"Because I was watching," I cried out.

"Watching what?" The smacks were coming more quickly now, stinging, landing relentlessly on the same spot. My ass burned. I tried to wriggle away from the aim of her blows, but to no avail. "Answer me: You were watching what?"

"I was watching Daddy fuck you."

"And what else were you doing?"

She pulled gently but firmly on my hair, forcing me to look up into her face. "And what else were you doing?" she asked again, her eyes nearly glowing with lust.

"I was touching myself," I said.

"Don't tell me, tell Daddy."

Daddy had gotten off the bed and come around to the front of me. He was slowly jerking himself off in my face. I looked up at him now too. God, he looked hot. I confessed to him in my tiniest voice, "I was touching myself while I watched you fuck her."

Daddy seemed to be in a swoon. He stuck the head of his

cock between my lips. Arching my head back uncomfortably, he worked his thick tool in and out of my mouth.

Louise worked two fingers up my hole then, giving me a thorough finger fucking while Daddy worked on my eager mouth. Within moments, Daddy had pulled a condom from his pocket.

"It's Daddy's turn to punish you now," he explained. "I want you to kneel on the edge of the bed and lick Louise's pussy." He slathered some gooey lube on his sheathed dick. "You're to lick her until she comes, you understand me? No fingers, just lick her. Lick her while Daddy punishes you."

I understood. Louise was lying flat across the bed now, and I knelt between her spread legs. I began licking her swollen pussy with gusto, centering on her tiny, erect clit.

But Daddy's idea of punishment was sublime. As I knelt between Louise's legs, my smarting red ass at the edge of the bed, my panties around my knees, and my schoolgirl uniform shoved up around my waist, Daddy reamed my ass. He went at my hole aggressively, going in deep and pulling out slow, thoroughly opening the hole, giving me the fucking of my life.

It was my turn to moan into Louise's snatch while she writhed around on my tongue. She kept my face pressed close to her mound while my tongue licked furiously at her clit. It didn't take much to make her come. Daddy was grunting, seriously riding my ass in the depths of his own orgasm, when Louise came in my mouth. I came just moments after she did, feeling positively delirious.

But the downside of it all was that shortly after this little explosion of mutual climaxes, they paid me my fee and told me I was free to go—even though it was obvious that they were in no hurry to leave themselves. That's when Mr. Santos's opinion of our relationship became brutally clear to me. I was still just a hooker to him, if one he had an unusual amount of fun with.

It had been a rude awakening for me, one that made me less inclined to arrange many trysts with him afterward. I never let on to him that Mrs. Hamilton had once been my high school teacher or that it had been an unnerving liaison for me in a number of ways. I kept my thoughts to myself and went through the motions of earning my 500 bucks from him. Eventually, I stopped seeing him altogether.

But yesterday, watching his casket disappear into the back of the hearse as I stood in the chill of the drizzling rain, I wished I'd spent just a little more time fucking him. I was going to miss that guy.

muriel the magnificent

When Muriel Bing was seven years old, in the course of a single Saturday afternoon something happened that shifted the topography of her secret inner landscape forever. The day had started out harmlessly enough: an afternoon in late spring, close to the end of her second-grade school year. In high spirits, she and Tommy Decker, the little brown-haired boy whose family's backyard adjoined hers, played together on her brightly colored swing set. Higher and higher they swung, until Tommy wagered with Muriel: "I'll bet you can't swing as high as me and jump when I yell 'jump.'"

"Yes, I can."

"No, you can't."

"I can too!"

"Okay," hollered Tommy, the bet under way. "The loser has to do whatever the winner says," he shouted.

Muriel's sturdy legs pumped determinedly as her swing kept pace with Tommy's, her long auburn braids flying out behind her on the upswing then smacking lightly against her shoulders as she swung down and back. Over and over, higher she climbed, until Muriel had reached an exhilarating height.

"Now! Jump!" Tommy Decker cried as he flung himself free of the swing, soaring several feet out over the small backyard, landing in a tumble on the cool green grass, his empty swing chink-chinking to a sudden halt behind him.

Muriel, however, hadn't jumped. The sheer height she'd reached had been too daunting. When it came time for her fingers to release their tight grip on the chains of her high-flying swing, when her eyes had taken in the full scope of empty sky she'd be forced to sail out into and the hard expanse of ground beneath her, Muriel's bowels had clenched tight. She'd been too timid to jump.

Her feet dragged the swing to a stumbling stop. Tommy had already leapt to his feet and come running over, his eyes bright with triumph. "You lose, Muriel," he cried gleefully. "I won. Now you have to do whatever I say!"

Tommy Decker was only one Decker from a veritable sea of Decker boys. Unlike the Bing family, the Deckers were Catholics who'd had nothing but sons. In the Decker house, there were always boys as far as Tommy's blue eyes could see: In his bedroom at night there were boys, in the morning at the kitchen table, or in front of the television set when he came home from school—nothing but brothers. Tommy was drawn to Muriel Bing because she was an only child, a sweet, kind, and smart little girl, but mostly because she was just that: a girl.

"Now you have to come behind the garage with me," Tommy announced.

Bravely, Muriel slid off her swing, knowing Tommy was fully capable of making her do something awful. Once, the summer before, he'd plucked a carrot from her father's vegetable patch, a carrot no bigger than Muriel's pinkie, and had forced her to eat it, then and there, dirt and all. Another time, he'd made her shuck unripe peas from their pods and eat them raw, which gave her a churning stomachache. Worse yet, Mr. Bing didn't like Muriel and Tommy making a mess of his garden. He'd said as much, in no uncertain terms, on several occasions.

With a cursory glance back toward her house to see if anyone was watching her, Muriel followed Tommy behind the garage to her father's vegetable patch, her childish curiosity outweighing her reluctance as usual.

When the pair were safely ensconced between the row of hedges that lined the edge of the Decker yard and the garden at the back of the Bings' garage, Tommy told Muriel, "Pull down your pants."

She was stunned. "What?"

"I said, pull down your pants. You have to do it because you have to do anything I say."

Muriel stared at Tommy uneasily and did nothing.

"Come on," he persisted. "Do it. I just want to see."

In an unfamiliar mix of interest and fear, Muriel did what Tommy said. She unzipped her pants, tugging them down just a little bit.

"Those too," he insisted, pointing at her cotton underpants.

Muriel hesitated, "No," she refused quietly.

"Come on, Muriel, just for one second. Just until I count 'one Mississippi,' then you can pull them back up, okay?"

Muriel considered Tommy's offer, her cautious hesitation giving way to a growing intrigue. She liked the way it felt, Tommy staring at her underpants in earnest, and she suddenly felt eager to show him what she knew the sisterless boy wanted to see. When she tugged her underpants down just enough to reveal her smooth mound and the pouting cleft at its base, the expression of wonder on Tommy's face made Muriel almost burst with pride.

He was so entranced by the sight of the strange nakedness that peeked out from between Muriel's legs, Tommy forgot to count "one Mississippi." In fact, the two of them stood transfixed by the magnetic pull between them for several uninterrupted moments. When they finally were interrupted, though, it happened in the worst possible way: An unsuspecting Mr. Bing rounded the corner of the garage.

"Muriel Bing, what do you think you're doing?" he sputtered, as Tommy Decker took off running for the relative safety of his own backyard.

Muriel's seven-year-old mind knew instinctively that she had no satisfactory answer to her father's question. "I'm not doing anything," she replied weakly, hastily tugging her pants and underpants back up around her waist.

No sooner were her clothes in order than Muriel's father grabbed her abruptly by her little arm, escorting her up to the house, in through the kitchen door, down the hallway, and into her room.

"You know better than that, Muriel!" he practically shouted. "What was going on out there?"

"Nothing," she replied timidly, realizing in a panic that the most dreaded punishment was befalling her. The pants and underpants she'd pulled up to her waist only moments before were coming down again, quickly, and her father was pulling her over his knee.

"Daddy, don't!" she cried feebly, as the spanking got underway. But there was no stopping Mr. Bing. The smacks rained down on Muriel's bare bottom furiously as he unleashed a litany of reasons why what Muriel had done was bad, bad, bad.

This degree of anger was uncommon in Muriel's father, and she was unnerved by it. It wasn't so much the severity of the spanking that wounded her; she was pierced to the core by the sound of his words.

"I'm thoroughly ashamed of you, Muriel," he declared as he unceremoniously yanked her from his lap when the spanking was over. "What made you do a dirty thing like that?"

He stood her helplessly in front of him while he continued to lecture her harshly about the wickedness of her immodesty. Throughout the entire scolding, poor Muriel's pants remained around her knees. The little mound whose unveiling had so recently filled her with pride was now uncomfortably on display, the obtrusive source of her newfound shame.

❧

At thirty-seven, Muriel Bing, Esq., was as bony as a little bird; her modest breasts, her slender waist, and her narrow hips were always concealed beneath the finely tailored yet conservative dress suits she wore every day to the law office where she specialized in real estate. She wore simple silk blouses, buttoned to her throat, and durable navy pumps on her small, sturdy feet.

Muriel lived alone in a well-appointed apartment in midtown Manhattan and almost never dated. She was no longer a virgin—she wasn't as pathetic as that—but she had become an expert at repressing any unseemly urges to satisfy her impulses. Not just the biological urges, but the appetites of all her senses. She ate plain, unseasoned foods cooked at home, almost never drank alcohol, not even wine, and her spotless apartment held no aromas of daily living except for the distinct odor of antibacterial cleanser.

The law firm where Muriel had been employed since she'd passed the New York bar exam, eleven years earlier was a prestigious, well-equipped, state-of-the-art office on Fifty-Seventh street, just off Fifth Avenue. Each employee's desk had the latest-model computer. They were online, networked, firewalled, intranetted, and secure on their dedicated server. No software program could be accessed without a valid password. Outside meetings took place in the form of online video conferencing. Office e-mail was monitored and noted in extensive personnel files.

At home, Muriel's fondness for technology lagged far behind the firm's. She had a reasonably respectable computer and a modest printer, and until recently the only software she'd deemed necessary was for word processing, which she did a great deal of late into the night. But gradually, the outside world had caught up with her. Only days before, Muriel had upgraded to a high-speed unit with all the frills, even free Internet access—a needless temptation Muriel had previously resisted. The only e-mail correspondence she'd previously engaged in was work-related, and so it stayed on the computer at the firm. Still, acquiescing to the advancement of technology into the privacy of her own home, Muriel logged on to the Internet and set up her first personal account.

Her free Internet access included the option of maintaining a small home page. At first, she dismissed it out of hand, feeling no need to display any part of her private life on something as public as a home page. Yet, after some consideration, it occurred to Muriel that it could help advertise the law firm. She set about learning the software to upload a humble Web page devoted to her occupation as real estate lawyer, listing her experience and the contact information of the office and nothing more.

It was quite late on a Friday evening when Muriel uploaded the newly created page to her allotted space on the server. After she'd been alerted that the files had been sent successfully, she typed the URL of her home page into the address locator and waited for her handiwork to load into her browser.

It seemed like she waited a long time. The simple page was loading very slowly, too slowly, as if it were laden with images or those space-consuming enhancements that frequently tried her patience on other Web sites.

Muriel walked away from her computer and went to the kitchen to peruse the contents of her refrigerator. While the browser continued to load her home page, Muriel reached for an apple and a diet ginger ale.

è

In a particularly hot pink hue, the words "Muriel the Magnificent" blinked on and off incessantly on a pitch-black background.

Muriel stared at her monitor, first in confusion, then in complete indignation, as JPEG after JPEG of a thoroughly naked woman in all sorts of obscene poses assaulted her vision. Clearly she had mistyped the URL. She checked the address in her browser against the address she'd been given by her service provider. It was the same.

She was slightly panic-stricken, since she had no ready faculties for processing lascivious feelings, and the lewd images veritably bursting before her eyes in a riotous array of digitized colors were arousing something primitive in her, Muriel hurriedly closed the page and prepared to resend her files to the server.

Carefully, she reentered the FTP information, being especially observant about entering her user name and password. When the files had again been successfully sent, Muriel retyped her URL into the browser in a second attempt to load her home page.

This time it took only a few seconds for the page to reload. "Muriel the Magnificent" flashed merrily on the screen.

A decidedly buxom, fleshy, full-figured woman in a myriad of widespread poses, bending-over poses, and poses in which her substantial boobs were squeezed together tightly—these assorted sordid images greeted Muriel again.

It must have something to do with our names being similar, Muriel decided. Perhaps there was a mix-up on the server because of that.

Yet there was something oddly familiar about this other Muriel, with the teased auburn hair, heavily made-up eyes, and glossy lips, wearing spiked heels and little else. Muriel scrolled down the page to the final photo: The voluptuous woman was bending over, lustily grabbing a sizable portion of her rear end in each of her well-manicured hands. Across the photo, just below a protuberance of shaved labial lips, the words "let's make contact" flashed annoyingly, pointing to an e-mail link.

Muriel clicked on it, and to her horror the preprogrammed e-mail address turned out to be her own.

Should I? she wondered. *If I do, what will I say?*

Muriel didn't want to make actual contact with this other Muriel, but she did want to know where the e-mail would ultimately arrive.

She typed the words "Testing 1,2,3" into the body of the e-mail and clicked "Send," only to receive an e-mail several moments later notifying her that her test was undeliverable as addressed.

"But how could I have received *this* e-mail if my e-mail address is incorrect?" Muriel demanded of her monitor in vain.

Anxiously, she dialed the number for twenty-four-hour tech support. It was late enough on a Friday night that she wasn't on hold for more than two minutes. After having explained her peculiar problem to the tech support person, he offered to go to her home page himself.

"There's some information about a law firm," he said. "And some résumé or something for a real estate lawyer—is that what you're getting?"

"That's what I'd *like* to be getting," Muriel whined incredulously, "but what I'm getting is pornography!"

The tech support person was silent for a moment. "I don't know what to tell you, ma'am. There's nothing pornographic about what I'm seeing here." And he read aloud, verbatim, the brief description she had composed. Muriel was dumbfounded.

"Well, what am I supposed to do about all this pornography?!" By now, Muriel was nearly hysterical. "I want to see my home page. What if other people see these disgusting photos and assume it's me? That I'm *that* Muriel?"

Another uneasy silence came from the other end of the line. "I don't know, ma'am. I don't know what to tell you. Perhaps you should try to contact this other woman."

"But her e-mail address is the same as mine—and it doesn't work!"

"What do you mean, it doesn't work?"

"I tried sending an e-mail to her, but it came back as undeliverable."

"Well, maybe it's a dead Web site. It happens all the time."

"No, you don't understand. It's *my* e-mail address. It works just fine."

"I'm sorry, ma'am, I really don't know what else to tell you." The tone of the young man's voice was now edging into patronizing impatience.

Muriel slammed down the phone. "You useless piece of—" Then she fumed silently for several minutes over her first encounter with online tech support.

ॐ

Muriel stood rigidly in the hot shower, letting the water blast down on the back of her neck, hoping it would soothe her agitated brain. Her eyes closed in defeat and she sighed.

I must have sounded completely insane, she realized as her conversation with tech support reverberated in her head. What the hell is going on with that computer?

In a burst of rage, Muriel had shut down the machine, overwhelmed by the extent of her unmitigated confusion. She'd elected to give it up for the time being and prepare for bed. Her anger had followed her from room to room as she'd switched off the lights, secured the apartment, stripped off her clothes, and gotten into the shower, but she was determined not to let the anxiety follow her into bed. Muriel was prone to bouts of insomnia, a state of mind she dreaded.

In a white cotton nightgown and a pair of equally white cotton panties, Muriel slid into bed. The sheets felt cool against her skin. Muriel felt noticeably calmer. With luck, she would sleep.

At 3 A.M., Muriel's eyes opened. She stared blankly into the darkness and the first thought that commanded her attention was this: Why were so many grown women determined to look like parodies of little girls?

Muriel couldn't help thinking about that other Muriel; Muriel the Magnificent, with her womanly figure and shaved labia. It was absurd-looking.

Muriel snuggled more comfortably into her pillow, her hand absently playing at the stray strands of pubic hairs that poked through the leg bands of her cotton panties. As far back as she could remember, Muriel had had a generous thatch of dark brown pubic hair. She couldn't recall a time when she didn't have it.

Wait, she thought, remembering the Tommy Decker incident. But in an instant her mind skittered clear of the discomforting memory, and soon enough Muriel Bing, Esq., was sound asleep.

❧

On Saturday morning, Muriel slept in. It was uncharacteristic of her to even remotely surrender to the lure of sloth. However, her bed felt so comfortable—a cool breeze blowing in gently over the blankets, and a bird warbling merrily on a sill across the air-shaft—that Muriel was lulled back to sleep before she knew it. When she finally roused herself, it was nearly noon.

She sat lazily on the edge of her bed, looking down at her loose-fitting nightgown, her skinny legs. The images of the other Muriel leapt to her consciousness.

How would it feel to be so fleshy? she wondered. What would it be like to always have one's boobs in one's peripheral vision?

She tugged open the top of her nightgown and stared down at her modest breasts. She tried squeezing them together in an unsuccessful attempt to create cleavage. She eyed her flat stomach too. Then she noticed with interest how her cotton panties covered her slightly protruding mound so smoothly. She wondered what she looked like down there, under all that hair. And this time when her mind served her up the memory of Tommy Decker, she let it linger there.

"What's with me today?" she muttered, feeling her hormones beginning to stir. Then she realized she was thinking about her computer, about how easily salacious images could be summoned from it. Why not? she thought.

She didn't even put on the coffeepot. She went straight to her computer and booted it up. She got online and went directly to the images of Muriel the Magnificent. This time, she studied the images intently. She found herself especially intrigued by the photos of Muriel spread wide, where every labial fold was blatantly revealed. There was one shot in particular where Muriel held her spread knees up to her breasts. Her tummy bulged enticingly in this position and then the smooth-shaven vulva seemed somehow more garish; even the anus was visible.

"There's something really filthy-looking about that," Muriel said quietly, realizing that her pulse had quickened.

As she studied the rest of the images, she fondled her nipples through the material of her nightgown. Then she discovered that the crotch of her panties was soaking wet.

"Jesus," she sighed. "Enough!" She closed down the browser and logged off.

But now she was too distracted to make coffee, so she decided to go out for a cup instead. She got dressed and went down to the corner café. It was a beautiful sunny day, with a hint of spring in the air. Muriel surprised herself again, this time by ordering a double latte and, at the last minute, adding a cream filled, chocolate-iced doughnut to her order! She couldn't remember the last time she'd tasted a doughnut and now, suddenly, she craved it.

Muriel sat down at a small table in front of the window and watched the people on the street walk briskly past. As her teeth sunk into the gooey pastry, her mouth filling with the rich flavor of fats and sugar, Muriel barely suppressed an audible moan. It was delicious; it was the best doughnut Muriel could remember tasting. She made a mental note to have breakfast out more often.

She shifted in the seat and caught the scent of herself. She was still wet between her legs. As she drank her double latte, her mind filled with pictures of the other Muriel's shaved pussy and spread legs. She watched the girls walking past the window and wondered which ones had shaved pussies concealed beneath their jeans or under their dresses.

This is crazy, she thought. But she loved the feeling of surrendering to the lusty pictures filling her head. She felt hypnotized. Before she knew it, her mind was made up. She tossed her empty cup into the trash can and headed home to her apartment, to her bathroom, where she was determined to shave herself.

&.

Muriel stripped naked and sat on the edge of her tub. By now, she was so aroused between her legs that even something as light as shaving foam felt incredibly exciting. The steel blade, repeatedly stroking her swollen mound, caressing it, revealing more and more of her increasing nakedness, drove Muriel to ecstasy. When she washed away the final residue and admired her handiwork in the mirror, she was thoroughly enchanted with the new vision of herself. She remained naked the rest of the afternoon, studying herself admiringly in the mirror, adopting many provocative poses, masturbating herself to orgasm seven times. When she had finally exhausted herself, she collapsed on her bed and stared up at the ceiling.

What good is it to look so inviting if there's no one around to appreciate it? she wondered, coming peculiarly close to admitting that she wanted a lover.

Suddenly, Muriel realized she was starving. She pulled on some clothes and headed outside for dinner. She chose a local Italian trattoria, an establishment that had been in her neighborhood for years but that she'd never once stepped inside.

It was early enough on a Saturday evening that the host was able to accommodate a single diner with no reservation without much difficulty. He showed Muriel to a small table in the corner. The restaurant was dimly lit, a single votive flickering seductively on every table, Frank Sinatra crooning out from the speakers.

"Something to drink before dinner?"

Muriel looked up at the waiter as if in a trance. The warm timbre of his masculine voice had melted into her ears. His dark eyes were beautiful, his shoulder-length black hair pulled into a neat ponytail behind his head. Suddenly Muriel wanted wine. Red wine. The best vintage. Maybe even a whole bottle. She'd drink what she wanted, without concerning herself about being wasteful for a change.

When the waiter returned with the bottle of wine, Muriel noticed for the first time that he was probably much younger than her, but she didn't care. She remained entranced. As he poured her a glass to taste, he seemed to eye her seductively, making Muriel wonder if he could smell her from where he was standing. She found herself hoping he could. Soon a busboy hovered around her with a basket of bread, then another came to pour her some water. A different waiter came by for her food order, and, later, the host was back to see how she was enjoying her meal.

She felt flushed. Never had Muriel been surrounded by so many attentive and attractive men. She returned to her apartment reeling from the thought of so much seemingly available masculinity in the world.

She couldn't resist booting up the computer one more time.

&

The page was loading slowly again. Within a few moments, "Muriel the Magnificent" was flashing on her monitor once again. Only this time, the selection of JPEGs had changed. Muriel felt slightly alarmed: This was an active Web page after all. Who was this other Muriel she was so voyeuristically enjoying?

She studied the new photos with acute interest, for now Muriel the Magnificent was no longer solo, she had a male companion—one who was remarkably endowed. In one photo, the companion stood behind her, clutching two good-size handfuls of Muriel's boobs, while his stiff erection poked up between Muriel's spread legs. The images became more provocative as the page continued to load. In fact, in one photo after another, a purely pornographic tryst between two rambunctious lovers was thoroughly exposed.

Oh, God, this is what I want, thought Muriel deliriously, as picture after picture assailed her eyes and her fingers worked tirelessly down under her skirt.

The male companion looked satisfyingly familiar—much like the waiter at the trattoria who had poured Muriel her wine, who had kept her glass enticingly filled throughout the course of her incredible meal. The same waiter who had eyed her knowingly, as if he were ready to scoop up a bit of her smell with his fingers; as if he were aching to taste her.

In one photo the lovers were passionately entwined, their

copulating genitals readily captured by the camera's lens. Another pose illustrated why Muriel was so magnificent: Her lover's substantial shaft filled her mouth to capacity. Still more shots showed the lovers performing intercourse in every position. The parting shot, of course, was a daunting close-up of Muriel's snug anus stretching to accommodate every thick inch of her companion's probing tool.

When the final image loaded in front of Muriel's eager eyes, she succumbed to another orgasm. Her eighth for the day—by far, a personal record. Muriel forced herself to shut down the computer and find her way to a hot shower. But what a glorious day it had been.

૱

Later that night, Muriel couldn't sleep. She felt too keyed up. Finally she gave up any pretense of drifting off to slumber and walked into the dark living room. Clad in her white cotton nightgown and white cotton panties, she sat on her open windowsill in the cool night air and watched an occasional taxi zip across the nearly deserted street below. From where she sat, she could see the trattoria closing. The neon sign blinked off suddenly and then Muriel watched several of the employees exit the restaurant together. Most of them walked away from her building, but one walked in her direction. Muriel's heart fluttered when she realized it was her favorite waiter.

"Hey," she called out quietly, surprising herself. "Hey, you—hi!"

The young man looked around curiously.

"Up here."

"Hello," he called back to her, seeming to recognize her immediately, even though it was dark. "What are you doing up? It's so late."

"I couldn't sleep."

He crossed the street to the sidewalk three stories below her window. "I was just thinking about you," he said, reaching into his bag and retrieving a half-empty recorked bottle of red wine. "I swiped this from your table," he called up to her, showing her the bottle. "I didn't want it to go to waste, but it's too good to drink alone, no?"

Muriel's heart raced. She couldn't believe it was happening. Her mouth opened and words came out of their own volition. "Why don't you come up? I'll buzz you in," she offered.

"Okay," he replied, seemingly unfazed by her ready acquiescence.

He must do this a lot, she thought, as she buzzed open the front door of her building and listened to his feet hurrying up the steps in the quiet stairwell. He sounded eager, perhaps taking the stairs two at a time. When he reached her floor, she stood in her open doorway waiting for him.

He eyed her thin cotton nightgown, her skinny legs and bare feet. He smiled, a little out of breath. "What's your name?" he asked. "I'm Antonio—from Canarsie."

"I'm Muriel," she replied.

"Well, Muriel," he said, lifting the bottle once again from his satchel, "do you have any glasses or do you drink from the bottle?"

ò

Antonio and Muriel sat together on the couch in her dark living room, a faint light shining in from the kitchen doorway. They were only on their first glass of the leftover wine when Antonio set his glass down on the coffee table and reached for Muriel's, setting hers aside too. He slid closer to her on the couch.

"You know, you look really inviting in that little nightie," he began quietly. "Do you ask a lot of guys up here in the middle of the night?"

"No," Muriel replied nervously. "I haven't even been on a date in I don't know how long."

"Well, that would explain it."

"Explain what?"

"You have this air about you, you know? Like you're really ready for it. Am I right?" he asked, his hand sliding up her thigh, under her nightgown, his fingertips brushing along the leg band of her panties.

Muriel caught her breath and didn't reply.

"What's the matter, Muriel?" Antonio taunted her, his warm hand slipping down between her loosely parted legs, then fleetingly across the crotch of her panties.

"Nothing," she managed to answer.

"Are you sure?" he persisted, his other hand reaching for the back of her head now.

"I'm sure," she said, her mouth finding his in the darkness and locking on.

He tasted like wine, cigarettes, coffee. He smelled of all the robust flavors of every Italian meal he'd been in the vicinity of at the trattoria. It was a heady mixture, an unfamiliar but not unpleasant scent for Muriel, because above all, he smelled like a man, and her entire body responded.

Antonio was all over her, his hands everywhere: under her nightie to fondle her nipples, then running through her hair as they continued to kiss, then down along her thighs, then grabbing her ass. Finally he tugged her panties down and discovered the smoothness of her shaved mound with his fingers.

"One of those naughty little girls, huh?" he whispered. "For some reason that doesn't surprise me."

In a mere moment, he had her panties completely off, her thighs spread, and his face buried between her legs. It wasn't the first time Muriel had felt a man's mouth on her down there, but it was the first time she let herself enjoy it. It was exhilarating. Antonio's tongue explored the swelling folds of her inner lips, then found her clitoris and lingered there while his fingers pushed into the sopping wetness of her hole.

She followed his lead effortlessly, her eager body assuming whatever position Antonio favored with only the slightest word of encouragement from him; positions she'd shied away from in the past because she'd feared the lewd postures were too immodest, perhaps even degrading. But now, as Antonio mounted her from behind, as she gripped the arm of the couch and felt his plunging erection filling her, she found herself suddenly grateful for the happy, inexplicable accident of Muriel the Magnificent and her lurid Web page.

Remembering some of the images that had filled her head earlier, Muriel found herself taking the initiative now. She straddled Antonio, impaled herself on his substantial shaft. She explored the length of him with her mouth, sucked his erection ardently. Then she squatted over his face and let his tongue go at her again.

Finally she invited him into her bed, where it was easier for him to pound into her relentlessly from behind, his thumb sliding into her anus while his thick cock tormented her. Muriel couldn't remember ever having felt so filled up, so completely appreciated, so thoroughly aroused. She took the force of his pounding as if she were born to be the receptacle of his fucking, his endless fucking, she never wanted to stop fucking...

Muriel and Antonio lay entwined on Muriel's bed, the Sunday morning dawn inching imperceptibly closer outside her bedroom window.

"You're too skinny, you know," Antonio teased her quietly. "We're going to have to fatten you up. Put some meat on your bones."

It sounded to Muriel as if he had intentions of sticking around, that he didn't consider this a one-night stand. She wondered how she felt about that.

"You should come by the restaurant more often. I can slip you some food on the house," he assured her, seeming to think she was thin because she couldn't afford to eat. "What do you do, anyway, Muriel? Where do you work?"

"I'm a lawyer," she replied.

"A lawyer? Then forget about it—you're taking *me* to dinner." Antonio drifted to sleep while holding Muriel in his arms.

❧

As soon as the sun poked through her curtains, Muriel's eyes opened. Antonio was sound asleep. She was relieved that he hadn't left her. Still, it concerned her that she was plunging herself headlong into such unfamiliar territory. Muriel had never done anything so rash in her life. And it had all started with that Web page. Her whole life had changed simply because she'd gotten online.

Then her curiosity got the best of her. It was uncanny how Muriel the Magnificent's experiences were only one step ahead of her own. She studied Antonio while he slept, then decided to slip out of bed and consult her computer: What erotic pleasures did Sunday have in store? Was the other Muriel still cavorting wantonly with the other Antonio?

The computer booted up and Muriel got online. The Web page loaded slowly, an indication that the JPEGs had probably changed. Muriel's pulse quickened; what was she likely to see?

"Muriel the Magnificent" flashed again, as usual. The first image loaded. It was Muriel with the other Antonio, and they were getting down to business. They were both facing the camera, and Muriel was astride Antonio with her legs spread wide, making it plain that Antonio's cock was deeply embedded up her shaved hole. But just outside of the picture stood another man. His erect penis was clearly discernible in Muriel's right hand.

"Oh, my God," she murmured breathlessly as picture after picture revealed the other Muriel getting lewdly penetrated in every orifice by two good-looking men at once.

"Caught you!" Antonio blurted, startling Muriel, making her jump.

She whirled around in her chair to find him standing naked behind her. She blushed. "I didn't know you were up."

"Hey, it's okay," he laughed. "Don't be embarrassed. Everybody likes to look at dirty pictures. This is a nice computer," he went on. "It looks brand-new. So you're online?"

"Yes," Muriel answered sheepishly.

"Me too. I spend a lot of time online. It's the wave of the future, right? Soon enough, everyone will be online."

Muriel looked away from Antonio and stared at her monitor distractedly. "Yes," she agreed quietly. "Soon enough, everyone will be online."

daddy's girl

When my little sister, Jenna, and I were eight and ten years old respectively, we fell in love with an older girl, Denise Dominic, our baby-sitter. Denise lived three houses up the block from us and was one of seven black-haired children in an Italian Roman Catholic family. All the kids on our block went to public school except the Dominics; they attended St. Christopher's and so seemed to inhabit a different planet.

Before Denise became our baby-sitter when she was fifteen, Jenna and I knew nothing about the Dominic family except that Mr. Dominic had a wicked temper. His dark Italian complexion grew even darker when he'd come out to his front lawn and holler for whichever one of his seven children had managed to fuck up this time. The rest of us neighborhood kids would scatter for the safety of our own backyards when Mr. Dominic was on the warpath. Rumor had it that he beat his children with a belt when they were bad—a thing that didn't happen in the rest of our white Anglo-Saxon houses. The unknown easily terrorized our immature but fertile imaginations.

Denise was a scrappy tomboy, even back then. It seemed like she was always in the doghouse for something. And after Jenna and I had fallen in love with her, it was particularly gut-wrenching to hear

Mr. Dominic's booming baritone holler out, "Deh-*nise!* You get in hear this minute!" Later that night, Jenna and I would hide together in the bed we shared and commiserate over poor Denise's fate, whispering in cautious terror, as if we were afraid Mr. Dominic himself would hear us from three houses away and, belt in hand, come after us next.

Denise became our baby-sitter when our regular sitter moved away. I was watching TV alone in the family room early one fateful Saturday evening when my mom came in, followed by a tough-looking, black-haired teenage girl with intense brown eyes. My mom said, "Jill, honey, you know Denise Dominic from up the block? She's going to be your new baby-sitter."

Well, technically, I did know *of* Denise Dominic, but I'd never seen her up close before. I was instantly smitten. From that moment on, I had an acute attack of butterflies in my belly whenever Denise came anywhere near me. Jenna fell in love that very same night, but her infatuation with Denise didn't last as long as mine did, which is why what came later seemed so incongruous to me—but I'm rushing myself.

Jenna has always been more outgoing than I have. Even back then, she openly flirted with Denise—baited her endlessly or tried to amuse her—whereas I was painfully shy and easily intimidated. I often felt like Denise barely knew I existed since my sister took up so much of her attention. But luckily, Jenna went to bed a whole hour earlier than I did. That last hour that I got to spend alone with Denise on Saturday nights was what I lived for all week long. Even though I rarely uttered a complete sentence to her, I pretended that coming Saturday would be the night I would finally confess my love to her.

The following year, my parents decided I was old enough to look after my little sister and myself. Denise had turned sixteen and wanted a better-paying job anyway so that she could buy her own car. My sister moved on to another infatuation—boys—while I stayed hopelessly in love with Denise from afar. By then it became difficult to catch a glimpse of her in person, she was so busy being a sixteen-year-old, but she filled my fantasies at night in ways that grew increasingly disturbing.

It used to be that Jenna and I confided in each other about our fantasies—especially the ones involving Denise. Remembering them now, they were only vaguely sexual, but they still led my sister and me to discover masturbation together. But as we grew older and Jenna's fantasies began to center more around wanting to be touched by boys, I still lingered over visions of being touched by Denise, of spreading myself open for her, of having my mouth between her legs, of being overpowered by her. I even fantasized that Denise was something like her father—that she would beat me with a belt, then expose and humiliate me and make me have orgasms in spite of myself. These were the disturbing fantasies that I couldn't bring myself to confide to anyone. Not even Jenna, who was usually lying right there beside me in the dark as the tormenting fantasies unfolded in my head.

One month before she was to graduate from St. Christopher's, something scandalous happened to Denise. I was only thirteen at the time, and the significance of the vague rumor I'd heard went over my head, but it involved Denise and some other Catholic girl in the shower of the school's locker room and Denise getting kicked out of school. I knew for sure that Mr. Dominic beat Denise so badly for being expelled from school only one month before graduation that she moved out of the house and took an apartment of her own on the other side of town. I didn't see Denise again for seven more years.

I had just dropped out of college and gone back to stay temporarily with my parents. I already knew I was gay—there were no doubts left about that—but finding a suitable lover was proving difficult. My first night home was a Friday, and I decided to check out the sole dyke bar in town, the Jack of Hearts. An unassuming, unmarked, windowless dark hole off a side street in the heart of the old warehouse district.

It was literally only a matter of moments before I spotted her sitting at the bar. She looked a lot older, but I knew it was Denise.

I wanted her more than ever. She looked gorgeous, menacing, so grown-up—everything I'd longed for in a female. Her black hair was chopped short. She looked lean and wiry in a black button-down shirt with the cuffs rolled up, a pair of blue jeans, and black combat boots on her feet. She was smoking a cigarette while she nursed a beer. My agenda fell together in my head quickly. First I would try to buy a drink without being carded, since I was still several months underage; next I would get up enough nerve to say hello to Denise.

I got past the first hurdle effortlessly. But just as I was getting up my nerve to walk over to where Denise was sitting alone at the bar, the incredibly femme girl who came out of the bathroom and then sat down beside Denise, slipping an arm in hers, turned out—to my horror—to be my little sister.

"Jill!" she practically squealed, noticing me right away. "What are *you* doing here?"

In as few words as possible, I managed to tell her I'd dropped out of school and had moved back home that very afternoon.

"You remember Den Dominic, don't you, Jill? Denny—you remember my sister, Jill, don't you?" Jenna looked at me as if she would burst with delight. "Denny and I are living together now," she gushed. "We have a cute little rental on the other side of the hill, off Main Street. You've *got* to come visit!"

I thought I was going to be sick. "Den" extended her hand to me. "Hey, Jill," she said. "Of course I remember you."

I shook her hand, looking into her dark eyes. "Hey," I choked. And I had nothing left to say after that. The electricity that shot through my bowels from simply shaking her hand made me so envious of my sister I couldn't speak. I left the Jack of Hearts shortly after that, halfheartedly promising that I would visit them sometime over the weekend.

Alone in my bed that night—the bed I once shared with my little sister—my jealousy festered. It was clear our parents had no inkling either one of us was gay. I lay awake plotting childish revenge. I'd spill the beans at the breakfast table the following

morning: "You two are so blind; can't you see that Jenna's gay?!
She's living in sin with that dyke Denise Dominic!" But I knew
that if the tables were turned, my sister would never stoop to
betraying me, so I managed to keep my mouth shut the following
morning and then swallow my pride and drive out to my sister's
house that afternoon.

Now, in hindsight, I can't decide if that was the best thing I
ever did or the worst.

I found their little house easily and pulled my car into their
driveway. The house seemed closed up, as if no one was home.
Maybe they weren't awake yet? I rang the bell anyway.

Den opened the door, looking wide awake and even more
incredible than she had the night before. She was wearing the
same combat boots and blue jeans, but now she had on a tight
white muscle shirt, which showed off her well-developed arms.
Her breasts were small and taut, her nipples hard and easily dis-
cernable through the thin cotton fabric. She wore a small silver
ring in one ear and had an unassuming tattoo on her right forearm.
A lit cigarette was jammed into the corner of her mouth. She
opened the screen door slightly and stuck her head out. "Hey, Jill,"
she said, taking the cigarette out of her mouth and staring at me.

She didn't move aside, ask me to come in, or make me feel
welcome in any way. I just stood there stupidly and stared back at
her. But what she said next was even more disarming.

"Jenna's being punished. She's been bad. She can't really have
visitors right now."

Her words were so unexpected, it seemed to take an eternity
for them to even register.

"Your sister's a little tramp, you know that, Jill?" she finally
continued after taking a few drags of her cigarette. "She made
Daddy very angry today, so she had to learn her lesson, and then
she got sent to her room. She's being punished—is there something about this you're not *grasping*, Jill? You have a weird look on
your face."

I knew I had to be blushing crimson by then. I was so filled with embarrassment, envy, lust. The whole scenario was dawning on me in rapid progression: Den was "Daddy," and Jenna, the lucky bitch, was being taught a lesson—maybe even the hard way. I tried to pull my gaze away from Den's penetrating stare but wound up focusing on her hard nipples instead. It instantly made matters worse in the envy and lust department, and I knew that all of it was registering on my face.

"You wanna come in for a beer?" she asked suddenly, looking down at her watch. "Your sister's probably been punished long enough. I'll check on her in a minute and see if she's ready to behave."

I was secretly hoping Jenna would refuse to behave so that I could get a little more time alone with Den. I followed her into the kitchen and she handed me a beer. She stood blocking the doorway, making it impossible for me to stand anywhere in the tiny kitchen except uncomfortably close to her.

"Well, Jill, you certainly have grown since the last time I baby-sat you."

"Yes," I answered as casually as I could, secretly thanking God that she was still a little taller than I was. It helped nurture my meager fantasy. Even though I was still disbelieving that my sister was actually gay, I knew I could never make a play for anyone she was involved with, no matter how badly I wished I had it in me to do just that.

Den stubbed out her cigarette. "What were you doing in the Jack of Hearts last night anyway: looking for love or just a reasonable facsimile?"

"I don't know. Either one, I guess."

"So you've dropped out of school, huh?"

"Yes," I replied, taking a sip of beer.

"You're very pretty, you know that?"

She'd caught me off guard.

"What's the matter?" she asked. "Are you embarrassed to be so pretty?"

"No," I laughed lamely.

"I always knew you were going to grow up to be very pretty. Jenna's pretty too, but in that over-the-top, superfemme way, you know? You—I can tell you wake up pretty. You just roll out of bed and look gorgeous, don't you?"

I felt like I was running a sudden fever.

She looked at her watch again. "Should we check on the brat now? I think she's been punished enough."

Not knowing what else to do, I followed Den to the stairway that led up to the small bedrooms. She stepped aside and said, "Beauty first," then followed a little too close behind me as I went upstairs. I could feel her eyes taking me in, checking me out.

At the top of the stairs, she passed me and said quietly in my face, "You have a great ass, you know that? I think it runs in your family." Then she put a finger to her lips and mouthed "Shhh" while opening the bedroom door.

I was completely shocked by what I saw. I couldn't believe it was my sister.

"Hey, brat, are you ready to behave?" Den asked as she entered the room. "A word of warning: We have company."

A blindfolded Jenna protested vainly through the ball that was wedged securely in her mouth and laced with a cord that was tied behind the back of her head. I didn't see the ball at first because Jenna was bent over a tall bar stool, her hair hanging down in her face. Her arms were outstretched, her wrists tied securely to two of the stool's legs, and her ample tits looked uncomfortably heavy, hanging upside down from her birdlike rib cage. She had on a pair of painfully high heels whose ankle straps were attached to the other two legs of the stool. Other than the shoes, she was naked. She had a tattoo on her butt that I'd never seen before, and her legs were spread just enough for me to see that her pussy was completely shaved. Something was stuck in her ass; from where I was standing, I couldn't tell what it was, only that it was huge. And she had bright red stripes across her backside, clear down her skinny thighs.

"These are what started the whole brouhaha," Den announced

as her fingers retrieved a pair of pink lace panties that had been stuffed inside my sister's vagina.

Jenna groaned only slightly as the panties were pulled out, but when the huge plug was pulled out of her ass next, she grunted hoarsely as if she were in pain.

My heart was racing. I was torn between feeling sorry for my sister—wanting to bolt before she could find out it was me standing there and realize what I'd seen—and feeling utter contempt for her because I was still jealous as hell. If it had been anybody but Denise Dominic, I would have fled.

Den unstrapped my sister's shoes, releasing her ankles from the stool's legs, then untied her wrists. When she slipped the blindfold from Jenna's face, Den grabbed a handful of my sister's hair, lifted her up by it, and said, "Look who's here."

It was then that I saw the ball in her mouth.

The blood had been rushing to her head for so long, it was hard to tell if she was actually embarrassed or not, but it was obvious that my sister was stunned to see me. She was unsteady on her feet when her body was finally righted all the way. She collapsed down on the bed and kicked off her shoes. She unwedged the ball from her mouth as she stared up warily at Den, who stood over her and said, "You want the panties now? Huh? How 'bout it, tough girl? You want to test me again?"

I had lived with my little sister long enough to know how she behaved when she'd been seriously punished, and the way she shamefacedly replied "no" to all of Den's questions made me wonder just what the heck had been going on between them. Had it been some kind of a sex scene that they'd both gotten off on, or had Jenna just been incredibly abused?

Den picked up a pair of scissors that were lying on the dresser, cut the lace panties in two, and dropped them into a wastebasket.

On her way out the bedroom door, she winked at me, grabbed hold of my arm, and said, "Are you ready for another beer?"

I didn't feel right leaving Jenna alone like that—especially

43

since I wasn't sure what had happened. "Maybe I should stay with her," I said.

Den stopped at the top of the stairs and looked at me. "Why? She's okay. She's just gonna jump in the shower. She'll be down in a minute."

I felt more confused than ever.

Then Den seemed to notice the look of concern that must have been on my face. "Hey," she said. "What's going on with you? You don't think I'd ever hurt either one of you girls, do you? Come on now. It's just sex. Let's get you another beer. I promise you, your sister's okay."

The fact that Den had even remotely included me in that statement jerked me right back to feeling hot for her again. I followed her into the kitchen for my next beer, noticing that this time she also took a bottle for herself. Once again she stood in front of the doorway, keeping me at an uncomfortable disadvantage. I couldn't kid myself anymore—I liked it.

"I'm sorry that upset you, Jill. I was just playing."

"I wasn't upset," I spluttered. "I guess, well, I just never expected to see my little sister like that. I never dreamed she was into that stuff."

"She's not, really," Den said matter-of-factly. "She's just trying it out. Experimenting, you know? She wanted to be my lover, so I'm letting her be my lover—for as long as she can take it. But she's not exactly a natural, by any means."

"Oh," I replied a little hopefully, in lieu of saying what I was really thinking.

"Hey," she said, moving a little closer toward me. "What are you doing this afternoon? Why don't you stick around? We have some friends coming over." Then, to my complete amazement, her hand went under my shirt, expertly found my nipple, even though it was safely hidden inside my bra, and pinched it. "Don't worry about your sister," she said quietly. "It's not love, Jill. She's just killing time. You'll see."

I wanted to kiss her, but nothing in her expression looked like she would allow it. She seemed content to pinch my nipple, tug on it through my bra, and watch approvingly as my pelvis began to writhe. "You always were the one who behaved. Look at you. You never gave me any trouble."

By the time my sister came downstairs, Den and I were sitting like normal people on the couch in their living room. Even though I was in a veritable swoon and not really aware of anything but my hormones galloping through my body, I somehow managed to make what sounded to me like reasonable conversation. Although, because of my guilty conscience, it was hard to look my sister in the eye anymore, I noticed that she seemed to be having just as much trouble looking directly at me, so I didn't feel quite so bad. And when their friends arrived and the liquor began to flow, I saw with my own eyes what Den had said earlier about Jenna—she *was* a little tramp, planting herself in another woman's lap and making out with her in front of all of us.

It was then that I saw Den motion to me to follow her upstairs. I couldn't believe my good fortune. We weren't even halfway up the stairs—we were just barely out of sight—when Den pulled me up to the step above of hers. "Take down your pants," she said.

"What?"

"You heard me. I said take down your pants. Come on, I wanna see your ass."

I did as she asked. With fumbling fingers, I quickly unzipped my jeans and lowered them down my thighs, tugging my panties down after them.

"Good girl," she whispered, grabbing me around my waist and pulling my naked ass up against her crotch. She reached down between my slippery labia, dipping into the wetness and sliding it all over my clitoris. I moaned. I couldn't help myself. Her teeth sank lightly into my shoulder. "You smell so good," she said quietly, sweeping aside my hair, her nose taking in my scent. "Kneel down for me, okay? Do it right now."

She let go of my waist and I knelt down on the stairs, tilting my ass up to her. She pushed my cheeks open wide and planted her mouth right on my asshole, her tongue coaxing the hole to relax and open for her. When it did, her finger slid up my ass and her mouth moved down to my swollen clit, sucking it in between her lips. It felt incredible—mostly because I couldn't believe it was Denise Dominic. Finally.

She stood up abruptly and practically dragged me up the stairs. "Come on," she said, "let's get naked. Let's do this right." She pulled me into the bedroom with her and locked the door behind us.

I stripped out of my clothes and watched her strip out of hers. Her body was immaculate. Lean, muscular-perfect. But when she turned her back to me, I gasped. Her ass and upper thighs were covered in scars. "What *happened* to you?"

She shrugged as she strapped on a dildo. "The scars? A gift from my father, from when I got kicked out of school."

"Jesus," I cried under my breath.

"Yeah," was all she said, taking me by the arm and directing me toward the window.

I wasn't sure what she wanted.

"Up against the glass. Come on, you know. Your tits; put them up against the window."

"But it's still light out," I replied incredulously. "People will see."

"Do it for Daddy, come on. I get off on it."

I watched her slather the fake dick up with lube. I got a funny feeling I knew where she was planning to put it. I wasn't sure I wanted to take that huge cock up my ass right in front of the window.

Den looked at me, rubbing even more lube onto the cock. "Come on, Jill," she said. "Do it for Daddy. Make me happy. I don't want to have to beg. It makes me angry to have to beg, and then there's no telling what we're liable to get into."

I thought of my sister battened down over the barstool, an even larger tool wedged into *her* ass. I went over to the window and did as she said, pressing my tits up against the cold glass.

Den was right behind me, her slippery hands prying me open, pushing the head of the tool into my tight hole. It felt enormous. I wanted to cry out.

"Don't," she encouraged me. "You're a big girl now, you can take it. I know you can. It hurts a little, I know, but soon you'll be begging me to fuck you like a dog, you know it."

I did know it. I tried to relax and take it all the way up without flinching. In a matter of moments she was fucking me savagely, stuffing my ass. It felt so good. I was oblivious to being in front of the window, my tits pressed flat against it, in full view of anyone who might happen to walk down the street. "Oh, yeah," I was ranting, "fuck me."

After a few minutes, she pulled me away from the window and tossed me onto the bed. "Come on," she said. "Beg me. Beg me to fuck you like a dog."

"Fuck me like a dog," I begged, assuming all fours as she mounted me, the dildo pushing into me again, filling my ass; stretching me open all the way.

"Louder than that. Beg like you mean it."

"Fuck me like a dog," I cried, as she pumped into me hard. "Fuck me like a dog!"

"That's right, Jill. Who's your Daddy?" she asked, slapping my ass.

"You're my Daddy."

"I can't hear you," she said, slapping me again, her hips increasing their rhythm almost viciously—I had to hold on to the bed.

"*You're* my Daddy," I cried desperately. "Fuck me like a dog, Daddy."

"That's good. That's right. That's what I like to hear." She plowed her full weight into me, toppling me over, but we stayed coupled, my asshole impaled. She lay on top of me, catching her breath, her breasts flat against my back. She smoothed my hair away from the side of my face, and her mouth found my ear. "Who's your daddy?"

"You are," I panted. I couldn't remember ever feeling so completely aroused.

"You want your ass to belong to Daddy? You want your pussy to belong to Daddy?"

"Yes," I whispered. "Yes, I want that."

"Show me how bad you want it, Jill. What are you going to do for Daddy?" She eased the dildo out of my ass, lifted her weight off me, and waited.

I didn't have a clue what wanted me to do. I acted on impulse. I turned over, faced her, pulled her down onto me, and kissed her mouth ravenously, wrapping my arms and legs around her tight, getting her as close to me as I could.

She kissed me back for several seemingly eternal moments. When we came up for air, I couldn't help myself. "I love you, Denise," I said.

It was clear she wasn't accustomed to being called Denise anymore. I was afraid I might have spoiled the moment.

"I know you love me," she said. "Your sister told me."

I suddenly felt like an idiot. "She *told* you? When?"

"A while back; when she and I first started going out. Hey," she said. "Come on, relax. We're here now, and it's working, right? Let's just see where it takes us."

But where could it possibly take us as long as she was still living with my sister?

"Just let Jenna play out," she said. "Girls like her always move on. She can't handle me and she knows it. What about you—you think you can handle me?"

"Yes," I answered, not entirely truthfully.

"You sure about that, Jill? I'm a mean motherfucker when I want to be. I'm a tough Daddy; I learned from a pro. He was the meanest motherfucker on the block."

"I know," I said, looking up into her face and catching a glimpse of a different kind of darkness, hiding at the edges of her eyes. Part of Mr. Dominic was in there somewhere. The full impact of it made my heart race: She was actually dangerous.

"If you behave, Daddy's going to be good to you, Jill. But if you play with me, I'll mess you up. You're saying you can handle that?"

"Yes," I said, hoping I sounded convincing, trying not to think about the day she would snap.

"Then we're good to go," she said, getting off me, her feet finding the floor. Then she grabbed a handful of my hair. Guiding me off the bed, she said, "On your knees, honey. Be good to Daddy, now."

I positioned myself between her legs and tried to reposition the dildo so that I could get at her clit.

"No, no, no," she corrected me, putting the dildo back in place and pressing the head of it against my lips. "Do it the way the Dominics do it; be a good girl for Daddy."

I took the huge fake cock into my mouth and let her find her own rhythm with it, working it in and out. I held on to her legs as her fist held tight to my hair, and a chill ran through me. "That's right," she chanted. "That's right, honey. Be good to Daddy and Daddy is going to eat you up. Daddy is going to give it to you the way his little girl likes it. Just as long as you behave."

And even though I was writhing over every exquisite minute of surrendering to Denise Dominic at last, I had a sick feeling down in my belly that her own Daddy, the formidable Mr. Dominic—the meanest motherfucker on the block—was even meaner than he'd looked and probably should have been shot. "Do it the way the Dominics do it," Denise said, forcing me to suck her cock as she had probably learned to do long ago. "Be a good girl for Daddy."

making whoopie

Evan's oceanfront home in Maui was a spectacular monument to modernism. Constructed in jutting geometric angles and utilizing windows of a massive height, it created the illusion—at the back of the house, anyway—of a structure with no walls at all. Evan could lie alone in the evening, on the great expanse of his austerely appointed king-size bed, contemplate the unobstructed panorama of sunset and crashing waves outside his bedroom window—eleven-foot sheets of sheer, uninterrupted glass—and feel as if he were the only living soul in God's universe.

The truth, however, was quite different. Evan couldn't remember the last time he'd been completely alone. Not only was Cheng, Evan's cook, in the kitchen directly underneath him preparing dinner, but Evan was currently one of the more famous movie stars in the English-speaking world. Beyond the tall privacy wall that guarded the street side of his modern edifice of concrete and glass, there was a never-ending parade of people—most of them curious strangers with cameras. Strangers by the thousands, it sometimes seemed to Evan, even in the relative remoteness of Maui. And within the hour Dorianne and all her luggage would be arriving from Honolulu, en route from Los Angeles. Evan might never be completely alone again.

This was it. This was the final hour. If everything proceeded as planned, Evan and Dorianne would legally be husband and wife before the night was over. It was going to be a small and private ceremony: the bride, the groom, and the judge, with Cheng and the judge's wife serving as witnesses. How they had managed to keep the news of the impending marriage out of the papers was further proof that when Evan truly desired to keep something private, it could be accomplished.

At the age of forty, Evan Crane, who had been in the public eye since his mid-twenties, had quite an impressive list of things he had managed to keep private—most notably, a long string of homosexual liaisons.

Dorianne was well aware of most of them; in fact, she'd even participated in a three-way with Evan and one of his male lovers once, back in Los Angeles. Evan had been impressed, even a little taken aback, by Dorianne's capacity for lust, her willingness to be accommodating with her mouth and to surrender her holes to the repeated poundings of both men. But ultimately, Dorianne had been left sleeping alone in the master bedroom while Evan and Giovanni had slipped downstairs to fuck without her, like voracious animals, on the living room couch.

"You don't have to deny it, Evan," Dorianne had spat the following morning after Giovanni left. "You think I couldn't hear you? All that carrying on?"

"Why are you getting so angry?" Evan had shouted. "I warned you Giovanni was insatiable. You knew it was likely to get complicated. I don't even understand why you agreed to do it in the first place."

"Maybe it turned me on to try two men at once, Evan. Did you ever consider that? That I might have my own fantasies? Or maybe I did it because I'm trying to understand you better. Would that be so horrible, if I cared about you?"

It was at that moment that Evan first realized he might be in love with Dorianne, that she might be "the one." She was fiery and not afraid to speak her mind. She didn't kowtow to Evan like everybody else did. He was turned on by her passion, by how she stood her ground, and most of all by how she seemed to genuinely care. Over the years Evan had learned some hard lessons about how to keep his ego in check and resist the constant temptation to have sex with every woman who threw herself at him. (Or every man, for that matter.) Especially since, though he'd just as often used his fame to score pussy and ass whenever he'd wanted it, he was frequently used by the people he fucked. They objectified him as a conquest and never seemed to care who he really was under all that fame.

Dorianne was not a sycophant; Evan had recognized this from the start. Still, during the first year he dated her, he'd always had another lover hidden somewhere, perhaps right in Los Angeles, or sometimes a continent away. He went through a whole pack of meaningless sex partners before finally realizing that he could better protect his self-interest by resisting temptation.

Even Evan's cook position had, until recently, been filled by a much younger man, James, whose talents hadn't been confined to the kitchen. Evan stared out at the vivid sunset and thought about James. What a little slice of heaven he was in the beginning, before he'd gotten envious of Dorianne, before he'd become contentious and belligerent, acting more like a spurned lover than an employee, and Evan had been forced to let him go. Evan felt his cock twitching beneath his linen trousers at the mere thought of James, though. Not that James was a better lover than Dorianne, but he had been incredibly convenient. James never seemed to aspire to anything higher in life than to suck or be fucked. Evan could summon James day or night and be obliged with a blow job on the spot. James seemed happy to be on his knees—on the kitchen tiles, on the bathroom marble, or out on the concrete lanai in the moonlight with the furious waves crashing against the black lava rocks beneath them. James had an eager mouth, and he swallowed without flinching. His devotion to servitude made him irresistible. It hadn't been unusual for Evan to wake James in the middle of the night; he'd obligingly turn over and pull down the blankets. He was always naked under those blankets, Evan remembered, always ready. And he didn't require any foreplay as long as Evan was sufficiently lubed.

Evan's hardening cock began to ache with the visceral memory of how effortless and uncomplicated it had been to fuck James. James would part his legs, raise his rump slightly, and let Evan mount him. His asshole always seemed responsive too; relaxed and ready for Evan's substantial tool as it plowed into him. James never protested. He'd lie quietly on his stomach and whimper a little, but he always gave Evan complete access to that tight, hot passageway until he had his fill of fucking it.

He glanced at the bedside clock now, trying to gauge if he had enough time to jerk off before Dorianne arrived from Honolulu. Evan loved thinking about fucking James's ass. It wasn't that Dorianne didn't turn him on or that she refused to take it up the ass; in fact, when she was in the right mood Dorianne could get just as filthy and take it just as hard as any man Evan had ever fucked. But getting her in the right mood for anal sex was sometimes a chore—she was a little intimidated by it. Evan was almost *too* endowed; his equipment, he knew, was huge. It was part of why he'd lasted so long in Hollywood.

Assuming she arrived on time, Evan figured he had just over forty-five minutes to get where he wanted to go. That was plenty of time. He pulled open the nightstand drawer for a squirt of his favorite lube, and the lone sheer stocking Dorianne had left behind last time caught his eye. She was definitely worth her weight in gold, that woman. She had such a nasty imagination.

Evan retrieved the stocking from the drawer and studied it, remembering how she had tormented him, using the stocking to tie his hands behind him, then bending him over the bamboo trunk at the foot of the bed. That night she alternated licking his balls with an incredibly well-paced rim job. She drove his cock crazy by practically ignoring it. Every once in a while she'd suck the swollen head of his shaft into her mouth or swipe a dribble of precome from his piss slit with the tip of her tongue, but other than that she focused on the rimming, her delicate hands keeping the taut globes of his ass spread wide so that his puckered hole was at the mercy of her mouth.

Evan knew there was no real reason to tie him up for a thing like that—it was something he'd have submitted to willingly—but he liked their pretense that he didn't have any options.

He released his hard cock from inside his trousers, slathered it with lube, and realized James was no longer on his mind. He was wondering instead what it was going to be like to be married. He knew that it was normal for the flame of passion to fade from most marriages, but he couldn't picture it happening between him and Dorianne. Only the night before he'd been half-crazy with lust for her, calling her at her hotel on Waikiki, waking her, insisting they get off together over the phone. Even though she'd been groggy with sleep, he knew the words that would get to her, trigger her hormones to flow through her like a river of fire, flooding her gorgeous pussy until she was wide awake and touching herself.

"Remember what it was like," his voice had caressed her through the phone wires, "that first time I took you up to my room, back when I had that house in the hills? Remember that, Dorianne? What a filthy little girl you were. You really surprised me that night. Remember what I made you do?"

"Yes," Dorianne's breathy voice had come back at him in the darkness. "I remember."

"Tell me what you remember."

"You made me lift up my dress and pull down my panties."

"And what else?"

"You made me get down on my knees."

"And then what did I make you do?"

"Unzip your trousers with my teeth and lick your cock."

Evan loved to hear the word *cock* coming out of Dorianne's mouth. She had a way of making the whole notion of a cock seem scary to her, scarier than he knew it could possibly be, but it made her seem vulnerable just the same. "That's right," he said. "You did such dirty things with my cock that night, didn't you?"

"Yes."

"Why did you do it, Dorianne? Why were you such a nasty little girl?"

"Because," she whispered, "I'm your slut, Evan. You know that. I'm a slave to your cock. I'll do whatever you ask me to do as long as I know I can have that big cock of yours in one of my tight holes."

"Oh yeah? Do I get to choose which tight hole I put it in?"

"Yeah."

"Even your asshole, Dorianne? You're going to take me up your tight ass?"

"Yes."

"All the way up?"

"Yes. Even if it makes me sweat."

"If what makes you sweat?"

"Feeling myself stretched open back there—your cock is huge."

They had gone on like that for nearly an hour. Evan hadn't been able to stand the idea of hanging up, of being alone without her in his bed, even for his final night as a bachelor. But eventually she insisted that she had to get some sleep, even though he hadn't come yet. "I'm going to be a blushing bride tomorrow, Evan, remember? I'm forty-three years old. I'm going to need all the help I can get."

Evan liked that she was older than he was. It satisfied his occasional fantasy of having an older woman take charge of him. "Okay, Dorianne," he'd conceded, preparing to hang up the phone at last, "I'll let you go this time. But after tomorrow I'm never letting you go again." When they hung up, he was alone in the darkness, his fist around his aching cock. Much like he was now—thinking of Dorianne naked, her long legs parted, revealing the closely-clipped black hairs that set off the fiery pink flesh of her engorged pussy when she was fully aroused, breathing hard and waiting for him.

Evan loved the sight of her like that. He knew from experience that she would cry out and clutch at his hair, his back, his ass, when he finally lay down on her, penetrated her, and gave it to her hard.

He liked to hear her passionate cries in his ear. Sometimes it sounded as if she were in pain.

His fist slid languorously over the slippery head of his cock as he thought about Dorianne and those cries she made. In his mind he replayed the night he and Giovanni had both gone at her—it was one of his favorite memories. She'd gotten especially worked up when she was on all fours, getting it at both ends at once. Giovanni kept a firm grip on her ass as he pounded his uncut meat into Dorianne's vagina. Evan's eyes couldn't get enough. He was on his knees in front of her, his erection filling her mouth as she grunted from the force of Giovanni's rhythm. Evan dug his fingers into Dorianne's hair, grabbing it in his fists while he fucked her mouth hard. He knew they were getting rough with her, but she seemed to be wildly into it.

Evan worked his cock more vigorously now, tugging it faster in time to the visions replaying in his head. He loved to think of Dorianne as a slut, as his own perfect slut, taking whatever he could dole out. He couldn't wait to be with her again—he hadn't slept with her in nearly a week. Tonight he was going to devour her.

They would be married then, he realized. Somewhere in the back of his brain the thought agitated him—what about the men, he wondered? Was she really going to be okay with his occasional men? They had talked about it. She said she would deal with it somehow. Bisexuality didn't just disappear because a person uttered some marriage vows. They both knew it.

Evan decided to worry about it later. For now, he wanted to continue imagining Dorianne getting good and fucked. He knew, for the most part, that she had loved it that night with Giovanni—she loved being filled up, utilized, put through it for hours. Evan thought about her, sitting on the airplane in first class; everything about Dorianne was first-class. He figured no one would ever guess—not the flight attendants, the other passengers, or the driver who was waiting for her at the gate. None of them would ever suspect that she was a woman who would prefer to be naked and on all fours, getting it hard at both ends from two men at once.

Mrs. Dorianne Crane.

Evan turned it over in his mind, thinking that the name suited her perfectly. Then it occurred to him that maybe she was going to keep her own name—he'd never bothered to ask. He'd try to remember to ask her later. Right now, he was concentrating on having her to himself, having her naked and underneath him; his swollen cock pushing into her vagina and feeling it open for him. He was so tired of fucking his own hand. He wanted to feel his chest pressed down against her soft breasts, her legs wrapped around him tight, her hands grabbing onto his ass and holding him down, grinding against him like she couldn't get enough of his hard cock in her hole.

He was very close to coming; he could feel the pressure in his balls when he heard her downstairs. Damn, she was either early or he'd miscalculated.

He swung out of bed and hurried into the bathroom to wash his hands, wipe off his cock, and zip it neatly into his trousers. *It was probably better this way,* he thought. Tonight his orgasm would explode into her and she would be in his arms.

Evan headed down the stairs and saw Dorianne in the kitchen, talking animatedly with Cheng. She was smiling; she was beautiful. *She's definitely first-class,* he told himself again. Evan hoped it would last a lifetime. He was going to give it his best shot.

safeway

There's no better place on earth for a bright red 1968 Cadillac convertible than the wide-open back roads of those barren desert towns south of Reno, Nevada. Or so we thought until we encountered all the dust. It flew up and pelted us when our wheels hit that unpaved road. It found our tongues and coated them. The dust stuck between our teeth; it stung, gritty and sudden, in our unprotected eyes. A desert is called a desert for a reason, we discovered. Choking and coughing, we hurriedly groped for the buttons that brought the convertible top back down and raised the electric windows.

Sheila and I were fools like that. We didn't give much thought to the elements; we just got in a car and drove. That summer, we'd saved up enough money to keep the Cadillac filled with gas for a month as we drove across the country and back. We had only enough money left to eat in truck stops and sleep in the cheapest motels. You know the kind: Truckers won't stay in them for more than an hour at a time. They don't provide you with a television or a radio or a phone; the owners spend most of their paltry income just trying to keep their neon sign lit. But at least the sheets are clean and they have running water.

This was early on in my relationship with Sheila, when our idea of a vacation together was to get in the Cadillac and drive for hours along state routes or back roads. We'd smoke cigarettes, stop for a cheeseburger, then find a cheap motel, get drunk, and fuck. Then we'd do it all over again the next day and the day after that, until we'd allegedly seen the country. But we weren't interested in checking out local color or visiting tourist attractions. We were content with finding the next town, the next liquor store, and the next motel room; mostly we were content with fucking.

Sheila was the first woman I'd ever taken up with who could make me feel almost petite. I'm big, but Sheila was even bigger. She stood six foot two in her bare feet and weighed in at 180 pounds. She was a strapping blue-eyed blond, an Irish Catholic girl from the Bronx. If you go by the notion that opposites attract, then we made sense: I was a brown-eyed brunet from Ohio, part city slicker, part hillbilly trash. I'd never set foot in the Bronx, and she'd never been to Appalachia, where most of my favorite child-hood memories had been born.

"You gotta be kidding me," Sheila had snorted when I'd raised a fuss about bringing the dildos. "We're gonna be gone an entire month!"

But I was adamant: no dildos. I had a phobia about state troopers. Just the words "state trooper" were enough to make me panic. Flashing lights, sirens, gruff men in Saigon shades. Even though I'd never received so much as a parking ticket, let alone a speeding ticket, in my entire life, I had this irrational fear of the highway patrol. Sheila and I would get pulled over, I imagined, on an obscure highway in the middle of nowhere, for no discernible reason. Our bags would be rifled through and the dildos discovered. Suddenly, my hands would be cuffed painfully behind my back, and Sheila would be knocked out cold by the side of the road. Then I would be treated to a forced sexual frenzy in the backseat of Satan's patrol car, my pitiful asshole penetrated violently by a state trooper wielding my own dildo.

"That means I can't fuck you for an entire month. What kind of vacation is that?" Sheila went on. "How can I enjoy myself, see our great country, and relax if I can't watch your eyes roll up in your pretty head and listen to you grunt like some animal in heat every night?"

"Sheila, enough. Man, I just don't like the idea of traveling with them, alright? We can get by on fingers and tongues for one lousy month, can't we?"

Well, it turned out we couldn't, but we were too far from the East Coast to find an adult toy store by the time we'd realized it wasn't going to work. After a week and a half on the road, Sheila and I finally pulled into endless, wide-open Nevada in the late evening. We'd had enough of vanilla fucking, and I, in particular, was squirming for something a little more fulfilling.

That's when we discovered the Safeway. It was a twenty-four hour supermarket: a brightly lit haven for slot machines, miles of beverages, and great slabs of beef. It was stocked with enough Hostess Ho Ho's to feed an army; family-size bags of Cheetos spilled out of its display racks. But best of all, as far as we were concerned, it had produce, farm-fresh produce in vivid hues unlike anything we'd seen in Manhattan markets, produce hydrated every fifteen minutes by a gossamer mist that showered gently from the top of the display case. It was enough to make us stare in awe—and get ideas.

"Isn't Nevada the site of all those atomic accidents in the movies?" Sheila mused, marveling at the enormity of the vegetables. "You know, where those giant grasshoppers ate Peter Graves?"

"I think so," I answered dreamily, eyeing the phallic cucumbers and a mound of huge, leafy carrots. "Have you ever seen a carrot this—"

"Clean?" Sheila interjected.

Well, I wasn't going to say clean, but she was right, nonetheless.

When another gentle shower misted the colorful vegetables Sheila looked at the huge, wet, glistening carrots and then back at me. Our eyes locked. "Pick yourself out a nice one," she said magnanimously. "It's on me."

My clit twitched. Sheila had looked at me the same way that night in Ariel's when we'd first met. She'd offered to buy me a drink but then had immediately stood too close and whispered unexpectedly, "Why don't you take off your panties?"

"What?" I'd responded in shock.

"Go in the bathroom and take off your panties."

For some reason her audacity hadn't repelled me. "Why?" I demanded curiously, taking a sip of the whiskey and Coke she'd paid for.

"Because," she explained with that look on her face, that look of carefully controlled and calculated lust, "I want you to misbehave so I can take you home with me and really give you something to cry about."

Remembering, I moved closer to her now in the Safeway produce aisle. "Maybe I should get two," I said softly, thinking of the little surprises she'd had in store for me that first night, once I'd finally discarded my panties in the ladies' room at Ariel's and willfully misbehaved.

"You mean one to put up your ass and one for the front?" Sheila asked.

"Uh-huh."

A woman dressed like a rancher's wife hurriedly tossed a handful of green beans into a plastic produce bag and moved far away from us.

Sheila and I kept our mouths shut after that. She stood by silently while I selected my two carrots: large, leafy ones with sturdy, rounded tips. On the way to the checkout I stopped short.

"What is it?" Sheila whispered.

"Vaseline," I whispered back.

"You're getting to be an expensive date," she said under her breath as we walked over to the health-and-beauty aisle. "You'd better be worth it."

❧

We were near hysterics when we got back to our car in the Safeway parking lot and realized what a conspicuous picture we'd made in the checkout lane: two rather large white women in black T-shirts, black Levi's, and motorcycle boots in the heat of the Nevada evening, buying nothing but two large carrots and a tub of Vaseline.

The little mouse of a cashier had pushed her glasses up nervously on the bridge of her nose, not wanting to speak to us or make eye contact while we paid.

"These carrots were probably her date for Saturday night," Sheila cracked as we drove to our motel room. "She's devastated."

"Well, that would explain her ill treatment of us. It wasn't contempt, just pure envy."

Our motel room was luxurious by our impoverished standards. It had the ubiquitous double bed bedecked with a brightly colored polyester bedspread, a ladder-back chair, a rickety desk, and a total of three dim lamps with yellowing shades. The pièce de résistance was a side table with two bright orange vinyl chairs.

Sheila went to the vending room for a bucket of ice and some cans of Diet Coke; I headed for the shower. The water pressure was surprisingly strong for a cheap motel in the middle of the desert. It was relaxing, so I stayed in there longer than I normally would have. When I finally emerged from the steam-filled bathroom, Sheila was hard at play with my twin dates for the evening.

"What do you think of a puppet show?" she asked as she introduced me to Mr. and Mrs. Carrot. She had torn the leafy greens off of one of them so that it resembled a carrot with a crew cut; she had left the other carrot's top springy and long.

"Didn't Mr. Potato Head have a carrot friend?" I asked. "Back in the dark ages, when we were both wee little lasses?"

"Yeah, I think so," Sheila replied as she fixed me a Wild Turkey with Diet Coke. "I remember a Mr. Green Pepper and a Ms. Cucumber, and I'm pretty sure there was a carrot too." She handed me my drink and lit a cigarette for herself. "Come over here and sit with me. I've been wanting to see you naked all day."

Perched on one of the vinyl chairs, Sheila motioned for me to sit on her substantial lap. She was still completely dressed; she liked to stay dressed until the very last minute. I was fresh from my shower and naked. I set my drink on the table and snuggled up close to her; we kissed, her tongue swirling around and exploring my mouth.

"How can you spoil such good bourbon with that sweet shit?" she complained after tasting the Diet Coke on my tongue. (Sheila took her bourbon neat.) "You try so hard to be a big-city girl," she added, kissing me again, "but you're just trash."

"I know."

"Only white trash mixes Coca-Cola with bourbon—hey, I was wondering, are you gonna be extra-special trashy tonight?"

"Probably," I confessed.

"Good," she sighed, playfully running her hand between my naked thighs. "You know how angry I get when you behave."

But I didn't know—I hadn't once behaved since we'd started going out. Our first night together—when I'd taken off my panties in a public place simply because she asked me to—was my personal milestone for misbehavior.

I'd let her buy me a lot of drinks that night. I had willfully drunk too much, in fact, because I knew she was the kind of woman who would stay in control. But I was a little afraid of her too, and I was drinking because I was nervous. She did unexpected things. When I'd excused myself to pee, she'd followed me right into the ladies' room, right into the stall, then forced her tongue between my teeth while my piss sprayed down into the porcelain bowl. She slid her fingertips between my legs and teased my clitoris while I peed, then she pressed a dripping finger to her lips and licked it. "I could drink your piss," she said softly. "You're that pretty. I think you'd better wipe yourself off and come home with me. Now."

I knew then that with a little privacy we were going to go a long way.

She let us into her apartment, flipped on one lamp, and then locked the door behind us. She tugged my hair and pulled my face up close to hers. "I have a roommate, and the walls are really thin," she explained succinctly. "Can I count on you to be extra quiet?"

I nodded my head and smiled eagerly.

"I mean extra, *extra* quiet. You see this wall?" She tugged on my hair again and led me over to the far wall. I tried to suppress an urge to giggle. "On the other side of this wall is a woman who's as big as me, and she's not going to like it very much if she discovers you're here. Do you know what I mean?"

I studied the wall, which had been brought very close to my face, and stole a glance at the rather unnerving expression on Sheila's face.

"I haven't exactly broken up with her yet," Sheila clarified quietly, "and technically, this is her apartment."

My bowels wrenched. *Holy shit,* I thought, *what have I gotten myself into?* But I was too horny to consider going home.

"What do you think?" Sheila whispered, pushing the side of my face flush against the wall. "Can you be extra quiet?" She swept my hair aside and practically bit the nape of my neck. Then she slipped a hand under my skirt and lightly rubbed my naked ass.

The wall felt ice-cold against the side of my face. I nodded my head uneasily.

"Extra, *extra* quiet, even though you know I have to punish you because you misbehaved?"

I nodded my head again, but Sheila gave my hair a tug. "I can't hear you," she whispered.

"Yes," I said softly.

"Yes, what?"

"Yes, I can be extra quiet."

She gave my hair another quick yank. "Even though…"

"Even though you have to punish me because I misbehaved."

Sheila grinned wickedly and let her hand slide up between my thighs.

&

I picked up my drink and took a sip as I got out of Sheila's lap. "You're a bitch, you know that?"

"Where the hell did *that* remark come from?"

I smiled at her and sat down on the bed. "I was just thinking about that first night you took me home and told me that lie about some huge angry woman sleeping in the next room who was going to want to kill me."

Sheila laughed in delight. "You were so *gullible*," she said with satisfaction. "You should have seen the look of sheer terror on your face. You were scrunched up against that wall and three of my fingers were up your ass, but you were trying so hard to be quiet. You were priceless."

"Fuck you."

"Hey, let's do it again."

"Do what?" I asked guardedly.

"Something really intense, where you have to shut up the whole time."

"Sheila—"

She got out of her chair and stood next to the bed, looking down at me. "Come on," she coaxed, clicking off the bedside lamp.

"Why?"

"Because I have an idea."

Against my better judgment I got off the bed. "What's your idea?" I asked uneasily.

"My idea is this," she said. She clicked off the remaining lamp and opened the motel room door. It had one of those old-fashioned aluminum screen doors, which was now the only thing between my nudity and the outside world, even if it was already dark out.

"Sheila! Close the door!"

"Come here," she said. "No one can see you."

"I don't care. Shut the door."

"Shh," she chided me. "No more noise from now on. I want you to be extra quiet."

"Sheila—"

"Hey, come on. Be quiet."

For some reason I did as I was told. It was an understanding

Sheila and I had between us: She came up with the ideas, and I went along with them. "What do you want me to do?" I conceded quietly.

"Just come stand over here in front of the door."

I let her position me right in front of the screen door. "I think I want my cocktail," I whispered.

Sheila brought it to me. "Don't worry," she said. "This motel's practically deserted, but let's pretend there are no vacancies and we have to be real quiet."

I agreed. I took a sip of my drink, the iced glass sweating in my hot little hand. I stared out the screen door into the darkness. The Nevada sky was clear, beautiful, and boundless. It seemed filled with more stars than I remembered. The night air had cooled considerably, and a gentle breeze filtered through the screen and made me shiver. I saw cars parked in front of two other doors, and light shone from behind the drawn venetian blinds of the occupied rooms. The main office was well lit. I could see inside it from where I was standing. The owner, a woman, was watching a small black-and-white television set.

Sheila pressed close behind me and swept aside my hair to find the nape of my neck. Her hands slipped around my front and tugged gently on my erect nipples. I reacted automatically, as I did every time Sheila touched me like that: I arched my breasts to meet her nimble fingers. But when she kissed my neck I had another reaction: I lifted my ass up high, as if I needed to be mounted.

My whole body squirmed under her deliberate, patient kisses. Her steady tugging on my nipples stirred the blood to my clitoris, and I could feel my entire mound becoming engorged. I pushed my ass back against the rough fabric of her Levi's.

"Oh, God," I moaned softly. "Let me put down my drink."

"No," Sheila replied. She began to kiss her way across the expanse of my naked back then down the length on my spine.

I steadied myself against the door frame with one hand. She grabbed my cheeks then and spread them wide, letting her tongue trail lightly over the crack of my ass down to my anus. She circled into the tiny hole, licking it tenderly, over and over.

"Jesus," I sighed. I tried to lean over slightly and set my drink on the floor.

"Hey," Sheila said sharply, smacking my ass. "I told you no."

I leaned over farther when Sheila crouched under me, her tongue dipping into my soaking vagina. I spread my legs wide apart to give her room. As her tongue worked its way closer to my clitoris, I felt her thick thumb pushing into my ass.

"Oh, God," I groaned. Keeping my mouth shut while she probed my ass was the tough part, and Sheila knew it. She spread my labia open with her other hand. She poked her tongue right into my quivering clit and licked it steadily while she worked her thumb persistently in and out of my tight anus.

My face and breasts were brushing against the scratchy mesh of the cold aluminum screen door when Sheila finally eased up on my hole. "Don't move," she warned quietly. "I want you to stay right there."

She stood up.

"At least take my drink, Sheila."

"All right," she agreed, "but only because I might want to tie you to the door frame."

Was she kidding? I looked up above my head. It didn't seem possible; she was kidding.

She was back in an instant with a pair of my nylon panties. She began to bind my wrists together in front of me.

"What are you doing?"

"Shh!" She smacked my ass harder this time. "Be quiet."

I watched in awe as she lifted my bound wrists up above my head, slipped the panties around the pneumatic tube at the top of the screen door, and tied me there.

"If you pull this thing loose," Sheila warned, "I'll really give you something to cry about."

I was still marveling at Sheila's inventiveness when she came back and told me to spread my legs. When I obeyed her I felt a glob of Vaseline slicked into my asshole. I'd been so caught up in everything else that I'd forgotten about the carrots. But then I felt them, both of them, their tips poised at the openings of my holes.

"Remember to be extra quiet," Sheila reminded me, her voice close to my ear. Then she pushed both of those enormous, atomic-size carrots into me at once. Not only were they huge; they were ice-cold.

"God!" I squealed between clenched teeth.

"Shh," she said soothingly, easing both carrots out, then sliding them in deeper. She worked them in and out, picking up speed, until I couldn't help but let it happen. I spread my feet wider and braced myself against the pounding Sheila was giving me. I started to whimper and moan, losing myself in the lust that was overtaking me but still trying to keep my delirium to myself.

Then, with a sick realization, I saw someone coming along the sidewalk: a woman. She seemed to be en route to the vending machines and would certainly pass our open door.

"Sheila," I whispered frantically. "Someone's coming!"

"Shut up and try to act natural," she offered as she hid, safe and fully clothed, behind me.

I wanted to yank my hands down from the pneumatic tube and at least cover my breasts, but it was too late. Here she came. I was quiet as a mouse, but it didn't help; she looked right at me.

"Hi," I chirped.

In the darkness beyond the screen door she looked like the rancher's wife we'd repulsed at the Safeway earlier in the evening, but I knew it couldn't be true. Surely my eyes were just playing tricks on me.

Speechless, the woman hurried past us.

"Sheila, get me down from here before she comes back!" I demanded. "I mean it!"

Sheila broke out in uncontrollable laugher. Though she obliged me in my state of panic, untying my wrists, she mocked me all the while. "Hi," she kept cheeping, her imitation flawless.

When I was unbound and safe once again behind the closed door Sheila switched on the light and lit a cigarette, still chuckling merrily over my complete embarrassment. I hollered at her: "It's not funny!"

But then I started laughing too because it *was* funny and I had to admit it. "Oh, man," I choked in disbelief. "What were the odds of that happening? Two lousy people in this rundown motel!"

❧

Later that night, when we had calmed down considerably, when we'd worn out not only my tender holes but our carrots as well, Sheila and I lay next to each other in the dark.

"Where do you think we'll wind up tomorrow?" I asked.

"Let's head south to Vegas," Sheila answered.

But we only made it as far as the Safeway.

operating in swingtime

Big Mike was a doll collector. Not dolls of the plastic or porcelain kind, but living dolls—the kind that wore skirts and racy lingerie. Crazy underwear, he called it. The crazier the better.

He parked his ten-year-old Chevy Cavalier in a no parking zone, tossing his forged police tag onto the peeling dashboard as he locked the four doors of the rusting piece of junk. He walked quickly away from his illegally parked vehicle and thought fleetingly about the kind of car he'd rather own, the kind of smooth machine he drove the guys around in sometimes when they needed a little privacy on wheels—a big Lincoln or a Cadillac, maybe. The thought of his inferior automobile prompted a familiar burning in the depths of Big Mike's enormous belly, setting off a succession of nervous tics: a grimace, a quick squint, and a sudden shrug of his right shoulder. But he kept moving.

He crossed 8th Avenue and headed east on 52nd Street. He hiked his trousers up around his fifty-seven-inch waist just as his beeper vibrated against his hip. He stopped and glanced down at the number. It was his number. His wife. He deleted the message. There was never a shortage of opportunities to respond to a page from Carla. He'd wait for the next one or maybe the one after that.

Big Mike wanted a new doll. He always wanted a

new doll whenever his beeper displayed another annoying intrusion from Carla.

The night before, at the 26 Club, there had been three new dolls. One quick one in a toilet stall—a blond who couldn't have been more than twenty-three, tops—and two from the dance floor. Those two had been the real deal, agreeing to leave with him and Joey and get a room with them at the New Yorker. There had been just enough dope to keep him hard until the sun came up, so the orgy now ranked as one of his more memorable ones. Why Big Mike had been so driven to suck Joey's cock, though, was a question he felt uncomfortable answering. He decided to forget about it, to blame it on all the dope, and he hoped Joey would do the same.

Big Mike opened the heavy door of Marimba's and stepped into its cool darkness. Outside, the spring daylight was waning, but inside, night had already come. The votives had been lit and placed on the empty, waiting tables. Night was as good as here. He hadn't been in the restaurant more than sixty seconds before Frankie started yapping in his face.

"Where you been, man? Carmine's been calling you."

"I was doing a tasting over by the U.N. We're going to get some new wine around here, Frankie. I'm sick of this mediocre shit every night."

"Do me a favor, Mike. Just call Carmine and see what he wants, okay? You make me nuts with all that connoisseur crap."

Frankie went back to the kitchen where he belonged while Big Mike planted his huge girth on a fancy barstool and made use of the house phone.

"Yeah, it's Mike," he said quietly into the receiver. "Gimme Carmine."

The bartender glanced over at Big Mike as he readied the bar for the happy-hour crowd. Big Mike didn't need to look at the bartender to know he was being watched, monitored. He always knew. A wave of familiar nervous tics washed over him again: the grimace, the squint, the shrug.

"Hey, Carmine, it's me. What's up?" Big Mike shifted a little on his barstool. "I was over by the U.N. A wine tasting. Strictly French, classy stuff. You would've been amazed. It was outta this world. I picked up a couple of Montrachet types...yeah, I know. So it's pricey, so what? You never know when we'll sell a bottle."

The bartender rolled his eyes, picturing Big Mike helping himself to a $200 bottle of wine at 2 A.M. when things were crazy, thinking nobody would notice.

"Which one?" Big Mike asked quietly. "Jimmy from Jersey or Jimmy Blue Eyes?" There was a long pause. "Don't worry; I'm on it," Big Mike assured him. He hung up the phone, never once looking directly at the bartender, who by this time was on to other daydreams.

Big Mike hoisted his ass off the barstool and headed for the door. "Tell Frankie I'll be back in a little bit; I have some business to take care of," Big Mike said. "Listen," he added, looking at the bartender now, taking in the full scope of his expression, noting it. "I'm expecting a woman, a real classy doll. Julanne. She was in the other night—short bangs, red hair, remember? You tell her to wait. Give her whatever she's drinking, on me. Just make sure she waits."

Big Mike thought about Julanne as he hauled his weight through the crowded street and headed toward the corner of Broadway and 50th, where Sal would be waiting. Julanne had been hot. Big Mike's cock twitched as he remembered Good Friday, what a surprise she'd been. He hadn't known who she was, but Carmine was feeding Julanne and her guests on the house, so he figured she had to be all right.

"I'm looking for a new doll," he'd said quietly in her ear, leaning into her slightly, rubbing her soft white shoulders as she sipped her wine. "You interested?"

To his complete surprise, she was interested, letting him kiss her on the mouth, suck on her tongue, right there at the table in front of everybody. Big Mike had tried his damnedest to convince her to go into the bathroom with him, to lock the door for a few minutes. But Julanne was not a bathroom fuck, and Big Mike had known it. He excused himself from the restaurant and gave her a lift home instead. There, in her apartment, he'd scored big-time. Julanne was a horny cocksucker. The best.

She was out of her little black dress in seconds. Her underthings were expensive—that was easy to see. Big Mike checked her finger for a ring, and there it was, shiny and gold, plain as day. Why hadn't he thought to look sooner? Sexing some doll in another man's home was a good way to get your balls blown off, but it was too late now. Julanne was unzipping his trousers, pulling them down to his ankles. She pushed him onto the couch and spread his huge legs apart. His erection was rock-hard, shooting straight out and aching. He couldn't believe the sight of her as she got down on all fours in that pretty underwear and started sucking his cock ravenously.

"Oh, how lucky," he'd said under his breath. "You're a good little cocksucker, you know that?" He watched her lips stretch around his thick shaft, her green eyes on fire, staring straight up at him. The tops of her soft boobs bounced enticingly in the lace-rimmed cups of her push-up bra. Her tongue urged the underside of his cock to push in deeper, and he obliged. Her talented tongue squeezed the throbbing head of his cock gently against the soft palate at the back of her mouth. Her tongue massaged the length of his dick. He grabbed her head to shoot down her throat—it was happening that fast—but she pulled away from him abruptly. She stood up and tugged down her lacy panties. She wasn't a natural redhead, Big Mike remembered now, but at his age he didn't expect anything to be natural anymore.

His beeper vibrated against his hip again. Big Mike knew it would be Carla, but he glanced down at the number to make sure. He noticed that his cock was making a tent of his trousers. He deleted his wife's message once again and thought idly about the coming evening, when he'd get another shot at Julanne and a chance to do something about his hard-on.

Sal was waiting on the corner. "Whatcha thinking about there, Mikey?" he grinned. "I could see that poker coming a mile away."

Big Mike chuckled, but he couldn't control the avalanche of nervous tics that spilled over him, adding a sharp sniffing action to the mix this time as he tugged his nose uncontrollably, as if he was coked up, but he definitely wasn't. He followed Sal into the office building and felt his erection subside. Making their way through the throng of office workers heading home for the evening, they pushed onto the old, creaking elevator, and Sal punched the button for Jimmy's floor.

Jimmy Blue Eyes had a cheap, gray, ugly office. It was plain to Big Mike that Jimmy wasn't happy to see them but that it wasn't a huge surprise either. The three men went into Jimmy's private office and shut the door.

"You tell Carmine I've almost got it. I'm serious, Sal," Jimmy said. "It's gonna go union; you just gotta give me another week here. You can't push these people any harder than I'm already pushing; you know what I'm saying? It starts to look fishy."

Big Mike sensed this was going to be a quick visit. He daydreamed about the receptionist they'd passed in the outer office. She was undoubtedly the type to wear crazy underwear. For sure. And impossibly high heels. Big Mike could tell this from a mere glance at the doll's mouth: the cheap shade of lipstick, the sharp outline of her lips. Her mouth was probably a complete waste of time—he could tell she would be a lousy cocksucker, too sloppy, but maybe she knew a cute trick, like sliding a rubber onto a man's tool using only her lips and tongue. Big Mike glanced out the window into the outer office and sized her up again. She would definitely be a nasty, nasty pussy-fuck. She was probably completely shaved. She was the type who would do it in a public bathroom without blinking, or even a utility closet. Without a doubt.

Big Mike's beeper vibrated again. "Excuse me, Jimmy," he said, coming back to earth. "Can I use a phone?"

Luckily, Jimmy directed him to the phone in the outer office, the one on the receptionist's desk. Big Mike stood over her, a little too closely, as he dialed his home phone.

"Carla, what is it?" he snapped into the receiver. "Again? What is it with you? I'm working here; this couldn't have waited? Yeah, well, I think you're nuts, that's what I think. We'll talk about it when I see you. Carla—no. Carla, I mean it. I'm hanging up now," he insisted. "I'm hanging up now, Carla. This is me hanging up."

Big Mike handed the receiver to the receptionist. "Hang it up," he told her. And the way she complied without even flinching made Big Mike revise his assessment of her. She's a booty girl, he realized now, seeing her up close like this. She will definitely take it up the ass the first time out. No question.

When Sal came out of Jimmy's office, Big Mike made a mental note to drop in on Jimmy's receptionist another day. Maybe around lunchtime.

"You tell Carmine I'll be by tonight around 10 o'clock," Sal said as he and Big Mike parted at the corner of Broadway and 50th Street. "What's Frankie serving tonight, by the way; do you know? Has he got those great little clams he had on Good Friday? Those clams were something, weren't they, Mikey? Did you try those?"

"No, I didn't," he replied. "I was busy."

"That's right," Sal remembered. "You left with that little redhead."

"That's right, I left with the little redhead."

Big Mike lugged himself back to Marimba's. Stepping inside the dark restaurant, he noticed her right away, her pretty red hair. But she wasn't sitting alone at the bar; she was sitting at a table in the corner—with Joey, of all fuckers. And he was sitting damn close. Frankie was sitting there too, across from her, probably watching her chew. She was probably eating something he'd fixed up special for her, something that wasn't even on the menu.

Big Mike headed first to the bar to pour himself a glass of wine—a Spanish Rioja, well-balanced, fruity bouquet. The flavors caressed his taste buds and then exploded, reminding him of how it had tasted to dip into Julanne's smoldering pussy with his tongue. The bar was brimming with happy-hour office workers now. Harmless silly goofballs, every last one of them. Big Mike kept his eyes on what seemed to be going down between

Joey and Julanne over at the table in the corner. Big Mike knew Joey well enough by now; he knew how Joey operated. The way he sat too close, giving a doll his complete attention. Propped up on an elbow, his chin resting casually in his hand. But Joey's other hand, Big Mike knew, was probably clear up Julanne's skirt. Maybe two of his fingers had already found her hole; Julanne wasn't the type to keep her goods barricaded behind complicated panty hose.

Big Mike clutched his wineglass in his large paw and headed over to their table. No rush. He wanted to see how they acted before they saw him coming. He knew the exact moment that he came into Joey's peripheral vision; he saw Joey's hand suddenly appear on the table and, at the same instant, Julanne's ass shift in her chair.

"Mikey," Joey called out to him. "How's it hanging?"

"Pretty loose," Big Mike replied. "Shove over."

Joey scooted his chair away from Julanne and made room for Big Mike to pull up his own chair and plant himself down at the table.

Julanne's green eyes flashed at Big Mike. "Hey, Mikey," she cooed, a forkful of pasta poised to enter her pretty mouth.

Big Mike could tell from looking into her eyes that Julanne was stoked, her pussy primed. He figured Joey was responsible for getting her so riled up. He hadn't been gone from Marimba's that long, though. Joey must have been operating in double-time.

"Hey, doll." Big Mike smiled back at her. "What's that you're eating—penne? What, in a pink sauce?" He turned to Frankie. "Is that back on the menu?"

"No, I made it special," Frankie replied. "There's more, though. You want any?"

"Yeah," Big Mike grunted. "Gimme a bowl of that."

Frankie excused himself politely and headed back to the kitchen. Big Mike watched another forkful of penne disappear into Julanne's mouth. He took a sip of his wine and then glanced at Joey. Joey was watching Julanne's mouth too, with a couple of his fingers pressed just under his nose, like maybe he was lost in thought. Big Mike figured Julanne's smell was all over those fingers.

"Mikey," Joey said suddenly. "Come closer here; I need to ask you something."

Big Mike leaned his head closer. Joey's mouth was at his ear. "How do you think she'd feel about a three-way? Ask her, man. I gotta have that woman."

"You mean right now?"

"Yeah. My car's right outside. We can hop over to Jersey. One of those places just outside the tunnel there."

"We can't risk going to Jersey, man, you know that. We got family trouble there."

"But I don't have time to get fancy," Joey insisted. "I gotta be somewhere later. Just see if she's into it."

Big Mike took another sip of wine, but it was ruined by the familiar burning that rolled through his big belly. The nervous tics unleashed themselves on him again, but thanks to the wine they were more subdued than before. Big Mike wanted this doll to be his very own, but he knew that was unrealistic since she was married. He leaned closer to Julanne. "Joey here wants me to ask you how you'd feel about a three-way?"

Julanne's fiery eyes told Big Mike all he needed to know. The words that came out of her mouth were just a formality. "I guess that would be okay," she replied.

"Where would you want to go? A hotel?"

"Well, we can't risk going to my place."

"No, no we can't, not all three of us. Well, you know, I have an idea. Are you finished eating?"

"You mean you want to go *now?!*"

"Yeah. Joey needs to be somewhere later. We're kind of in a rush."

Julanne's demeanor changed considerably. "Maybe another night, then. When we have more time to think it through."

Big Mike wanted to kiss her. He leaned his weight toward her and took a quick taste of the pink sauce that faintly flavored her lips. Then he turned to Joey. "Not tonight, man. She wants to think it over." He relished the look of frustrated dejection that washed over Joey's face. "Don't worry: She's into it. Just not tonight, man."

"Yeah, right." Joey got up from the table and walked away just as Frankie came back with a bowl of penne for Big Mike.

"Enjoy," Frankie said, then he returned to the kitchen.

≥∙

"Let's grab a cab," Big Mike told Julanne as he stepped out into the street and hailed one. "I don't want to lose my parking space. I'm gonna need it later."

A taxi pulled to a quick stop at Big Mike's feet. He opened the door for Julanne and then hoisted himself in next to her. When they got to her apartment it was the same as it had been on Good Friday: She was out of her dress in a heartbeat. Then she stripped him completely nude. Big Mike loved rolling around on her when she was still wearing her fancy under-wear. He tossed her down to the couch and planted his weight on top of her.

"You taste so good; you know that?" he said, kissing her mouth, feeling the need to devour her. His rock-hard dick slipped all over her silky panties while he kissed her. Julanne's tongue played with his tongue suggestively, making him crazy. He got off her then and settled into the couch cushions, his huge hand lifting her up, guiding her by her hair until her lips were stretched around his shaft and sucking his cock in.

He watched his thick erection slide in and out of her pret-ty mouth, her tongue always working it, licking it, stroking it—even when his tool was pushed deep in there, the tongue kept working. Big Mike reached his hands behind Julanne and unclasped her bra. He thought he was going to shoot when he saw her ample tits spill out of the lacy cups. But he controlled himself. He wanted to take a little time with her. He told himself not to stare at them, at how they bounced around when they were free and hanging down like that. But he couldn't take his eyes off them; they were incredible. As a safeguard against coming too fast, he pulled her face up to his and kissed her again, feeling her soft breasts press full against the expanse of his hairy chest.

"You want to go into the bedroom?" she asked.

"Does your husband sleep in there?"

"Yeah, why?"

"I can't do it, then. It wouldn't be right. Let's just stay here."

Julanne acquiesced, getting up from the couch and stripping out of her panties, keeping her stockings in place. Then she leaned into the opposite arm of the couch and presented her backside to him like a bitch all ready to get good and rutted. "Come on, Mikey," she teased him. "Get on there and show me what you can do."

He slid his thick cock into her snug hole and groaned. The slick walls of her hot, mysterious muscle stretched just enough to accommodate his aching meat. It felt like a vagina that had hardly been used yet—something fresh and young. "If you were my wife," he said, "you'd never be allowed to leave the bed. I would always be fucking you, Julanne. If you belonged to me, I could never stop fucking you."

He watched his tool slide out of her, slick and glistening, then he watched it disappear back into her hole again. She was light as a feather, almost. He had only the merest grip on her slender waist as he pulled her hard onto his swollen cock, let her go a little, then pulled her hard onto him again. He liked the way her gorgeous ass jiggled when he gave it to her hard. And the way she grunted.

Like milk, he was thinking, *but creamier.* Her skin was so smooth he could only think of words that would barely suffice—words like "milky" and "creamy"; stupid words. Julanne's skin wasn't anything at all like Carla's, he realized. Not only was

Carla olive-complexioned, she was also marked with scars and bruises, noticeable veins, and ugly discolorings. Too many years of frequenting dungeons and S/M clubs, he figured. Big Mike had no interest in beating up his wife and even less interest in watching other men do it. He almost never made the rounds with her anymore. It bored him. He preferred to swing alone now. And his refusal to participate any further in what she called her sex life had signaled the beginning of the end for Big Mike and Carla.

Big Mike's beeper vibrated crazily against the hardwood floor. He uncoupled from Julanne and found, to his dismay, that it was serious. "I gotta use your phone," he said.

❧

Shit, Big Mike thought as he lurched out of the cab in front of Marimba's and wave after wave of nervous tics consumed him. He tugged at his nose and shrugged his right shoulder maniacally. The slight burning that usually coated the lining of his enormous stomach was more like an eruption of lava now. Sal and Little Joe and the other Frankie from the Bronx arrived at almost the same moment. They all got into Sal's car together and waited in silence for Carmine, who was being driven in from Arthur Avenue.

At moments like this Big Mike wanted to wipe out every trace of his father, his father's father, and a long list of dearly departed uncles for having handed him this corrosive legacy. All it did was set up impossible expectations for Big Mike to deliver like his forebears had, but violence didn't sit well with him. When Carmine finally arrived from the Bronx, they separated into different cars. They headed for the patch of familiar wasteland along the Harlem River, and Big Mike thought of his legendary great-uncle Luigi, frying at Sing Sing in '22, strapped in tight to that electric chair while stinking black smoke wafted up from the top of his Sicilian head.

❧

Three hours later Big Mike heaved himself out of his own car, tossed the fake police tag onto its dashboard again, locked it, and headed down the stairs into the 26 Club. The three lines of blow he'd done in the bathroom at Marimba's had just about obliterated the echoes of those wretched gagging pleas a man held facedown in lye is likely to make. He was deep in thoughts of finding a new doll for the night, or even for a few minutes in the toilet stall, when he saw Joey at the bar, his arm already draped around a young one in very high heels. "Hey, Mikey," Joey called out over the music, grinning from ear to ear. "How's it hanging?"

"A little too tight. I've had a hard-on all day that I just can't shake."

"Well, say hello to Mary, no relation to the Virgin. You want to come get a room with us?"

Big Mike gave Mary the once-over. She was cute enough, but she looked like she was flying, totally loaded.

"Unless, of course, you'd rather be alone with me and suck my cock again," Joey gibed him. "What the hell was that all about last night anyway? You are one fucked-up motherfucker, you know that, Mikey?"

Big Mike succumbed to a series of nervous tics, ending with a sharp shrug of his right shoulder. "I don't know. My life's crazy these days. Carla's leaving me, you know."

"No, man, I didn't know."

"Yeah, she wants a divorce."

"Mikey, I'm sorry to hear it. Mary here can go a long way toward making you feel better, though. I know this for a fact. She gives good head, Mikey," he assured him, jabbing an elbow into Big Mike's rolling girth. "Not as good as you, of course, but she'll do in a pinch."

Big Mike grimaced. He ordered a double shot of vodka and downed it. He watched Mary, no relation to the Virgin, teeter on her impossibly high heels and tug at her pert little nose, her eyes glassy, like maybe her whole head was blown apart inside. Big Mike nudged Joey.

"Hey," he shouted over the music, "I think my own hand would be better than this doll; she looks like she's ready to pass out. Whaddya say, you want to go get some bacon and eggs? I'm kind of hungry."

Joey shrugged complacently, extricated himself from Mary, and followed Big Mike out of the 26 Club and up the quiet street.

the birthday party

I opened my eyes in the middle of the night, and at first I thought I was dreaming.

Danny was there, standing next to the bed, shaking me gently.

"Get up, Layla, I have a surprise for you," he was saying.

"What's going on, Danny? What time is it?"

"It doesn't matter what time it is. I have a surprise for you."

That's when I realized that we weren't alone, that there was someone else in the dark there with us. "Who's here, Danny? What's going on?"

"Relax. It's that guy from the bar, remember?"

I remembered all right, but I wasn't sure I'd been serious.

"You've got to be kidding, Danny."

"Don't tell me you've changed your mind. He's totally into it, Layla, and he doesn't even want the money."

"I'm more than happy to do it for free, honey. For a pretty girl like you."

I couldn't believe I was hearing it, that voice coming at me in the darkness. It was really happening. All that stood between me and my dream lover was my mouth saying that I refused to go through with it.

"Don't be scared, Layla," the voice continued. "I know exactly what you want. Danny told me all the details, right down to keeping the lights off."

I pulled the blankets around myself protectively and listened to my heart pound.

"Danny," I said quietly, barely able to get the words out. "I don't know."

"I'll be right here," he assured me. "It'll be perfect, the best birthday gift you could want."

"All right," I heard myself saying, "all right."

"Do you have the outfit, can you find it in the dark?"

"I think I can."

"Do you want us to leave you alone while you get dressed?"

"No, Danny. Stay here. I'm afraid of changing my mind."

The room grew incredibly quiet as I got out of bed and felt my way through the closet and dresser drawers in the dark. All I could hear was the two of them breathing.

I felt a little awkward dressing like that, as if I was overdoing it: a black velvet gown and high heels, my best pearls—all in the pitch-darkness. Knowing full well what was coming. I wasn't sure I could really go through with it; I felt too vulnerable. But I was excited enough to try.

"I'm ready, Danny," I said at last, "but swear to me you'll keep the lights off."

"I swear, Layla. I'll keep the lights off."

I sat down in the chair by the window, raised the blinds so that the dim moonlight could filter in. I smoothed down my full skirt and waited.

It seemed like an eternity that I sat there, my heart pounding.

"Hey, birthday girl," he finally said. "You look really pretty in the moonlight."

His hips were planted firmly in front of my face. I was afraid to look up at him for fear that I might see him too clearly and have a change of heart.

"Thank you," I said softly.

He knelt down in front of me then and carefully removed my high heels.

"These are awfully pretty too," he said. "Probably expensive, huh?"

"A little," I replied, still unable to find the full power of my voice.

His hands were warm as they slipped under my long skirt and then felt for the tops of my stockings. His fingers brushing against the skin of my upper thighs aroused me, and I couldn't help but part my legs for him. The crinoline lining of my dress rustled against him as he lowered first one of my stockings and then the other, sliding them off me completely.

Then he reached around me and put my hands behind my back, using one of the stockings to tie my wrists together. On his knees, his face close to mine, I could feel his breath on my face, and he appealed to me. When he finished tying me, he kissed my mouth, and as he kissed me, he pulled down the front of my strapless gown and exposed my breasts.

He kissed me for a long time, his tongue filling my mouth while his hands squeezed my tits and tugged my nipples. Then he collected himself.

He stood and had me scoot off the chair. "Get on your knees," he said.

Danny lit a cigarette suddenly, and the match seemed blinding.

"Danny!" I cried, startled.

"Sorry," he said urgently. "I'm sorry, keep going, Layla."

But the sudden burst of flame in the dark had unsettled me. It had lasted just long enough for me to catch a good look at myself on my knees, my most expensive dress tugged down and my tits exposed. But thankfully the darkness returned before I'd had a chance to see the face of the guy looking down at me. That might have made me change my mind altogether.

Instead, we kept going.

The man unzipped his jeans, and his erection sprang out full and hard. He grabbed my hair and guided my face to his cock. It felt warm.

"Go on," he said. "Kiss it all over."

I did as I was told, almost overcome with lust. I pretended that I didn't have a choice, that this good-looking stranger from the bar had overpowered me.

"That's good, that's right," he said. "Now lick it. I want to feel your tongue. Go all the way down to my balls. That's right, birthday girl, lick them good. Now come back up and lick the head."

I couldn't believe he was playing his part so perfectly. As he held tight to my hair he said, "Take it now, suck my dick," and he drove his cock in and out of my mouth. I tried to keep my balance, but I was unsteady on my knees, my hands too securely tied behind my back. Once or twice it seemed the only thing keeping me upright was his grip on my hair. My jaw was starting to ache. He was pumping into me relentlessly; spit was collecting in my mouth because he wasn't giving me a chance to swallow.

Finally he helped me up and led me over to the bed, where Danny was sitting. The man tossed me facedown onto it, but he was more playful than rough. Right away his hands were under my skirt, tugging down my panties.

I was so wet that when my panties came down I felt unexpectedly exposed.

When they were off completely, he wedged some pillows under me to raise my ass in the air. He shoved my dress up high, and I could feel the rough hem against my bare shoulders. Then he spread my thighs wide.

"Oh, God," I moaned softly when I felt his mouth on me.

"Birthday girl, you are so wet. You must be having a really good time."

His fingers spread my swollen lips open wider, and his tongue darted all over my clit. He licked me thoroughly, even burrowing his tongue deep into my hole.

It was then that Danny knelt in front of me on the bed and undid his jeans. He took his erection out and slid it into my mouth, arching my neck uncomfortably.

I sucked him eagerly, though, while the other guy kept licking my dripping pussy; while he pressed his face flush against me and jammed his tongue into my hole, his hands keeping my thighs spread wide. I could tell it had been a while since he'd shaved, but the friction felt good on my engorged lips. When he started to groan, I squirmed against his face.

"Oh, Layla," Danny was saying as he worked his dick in and out of my mouth, "you look so pretty like this, so hot. Spread out and wiggling your little ass. You look like you want to get fucked, you know that? You want to get fucked, Layla? You want a hard dick in your hot little hole?"

I was moaning crazily in agreement while I sucked Danny's cock, but my hands were still tied behind me and I had no other choice. I had to go at the pace they chose.

"He looks to me like he might be ready," Danny taunted me. "You want to get fucked now, Layla? You want to get fucked really hard? What do you say, birthday girl?"

At last, Danny took his cock from my mouth so that I could speak.

"Yes," I said. "I do. I want to get fucked really hard, Danny."

I felt the guy get off the bed. I heard him get undressed. In an instant he was back, his knees were between my thighs, and he had a tight grip on my ankles.

Then he pushed his substantial dick into my waiting hole. The full length of his cock going into my vagina made me cry out.

He pumped into me hard and deep, and all I could do was lie there, my ass propped up on the pillows for him, my ankles pinned to the bed.

Danny was back at my mouth, going at me in a brisk rhythm. I knew he was almost ready to come.

"Jesus," he was chanting, clutching my hair. "Jesus, Layla."

I was whimpering and carrying on from the force of the cock thrusting into me from behind. Danny jerked against my face hard and started to come down my throat. I felt like I was going to choke.

When Danny had finished coming he scooted aside and watched me get nailed in the moonlight.

I really started to sputter and cry then. The harder and deeper the guy fucked me, the better it felt.

"Oh," I was crying, "oh, God," as he pounded away at me until my spread legs ached and I thought he would never come.

When he finally did, I felt suddenly shy again. Everyone was coming down to earth quickly, and I realized I didn't even know the guy's name.

"That was really fun," he said while he started to put on his clothes. But when he moved to untie my hands, Danny intervened.

"Don't," he said. "Leave them tied just a little longer."

"Why?" I wanted to know. "What's going on?"

"It's well after midnight," Danny explained. "We're deep into the birthday zone."

"Danny, no," I protested, knowing him too well.

"Come on now, be a good girl."

"Danny, no, I mean it."

But Danny ignored my halfhearted plea and told the guy to sit back down on the bed.

"She's already wearing her birthday dress," Danny explained to him. "It's a shame not to let her have her birthday spankings too."

The guy seemed more than delighted to oblige Danny. He shifted me over his knee and raised my skirt once more while I struggled lamely to squirm away. "Come on," he said, slapping my naked ass, "you're a big girl. You can take it, Layla. A spank for each year. It'll be over before you know it."

"That's what you think," Danny laughed as he leaned against the headboard and relaxed in the dark. "Wait'll you hear how old she is."

on twelfth street

In the half-light before dawn the double bed jostles me from sleep; it shakes with a distinct rhythm, like riding the double L train from First Avenue into Canarsie. It's Manny jerking off again, I realize. Lately he seems to need this furtive sexual stimulation at the last minute before dashing off to work—strictly solitary sex is what he's after. Sex that doesn't involve me, that lands his jism in a T-shirt, which winds up in the tangle of sheets for me to discover later when I'm alone. And he says *I'm* possessed by demons. Nympho demons, the kind of demons his aunt, the Mother Superior, warned him about when he was a teenage Catholic boy in Buffalo. He's only twenty now. Six years younger than me.

Manny came into my life almost as an afterthought, like an unwanted conception late in life, and I can't figure out how to get him to leave. Whenever I suggest it might be time for him to move from my little hellhole on East Twelfth Street and find a home of his own, he punches me repeatedly and starts smashing dishes that are irreplaceable heirlooms from my favorite dead grandmother.

The one nice thing about this Catholic boy, though, is that he's so hung up on his Catholic upbringing that he's psychologically incapable of coming in a girl's mouth. I can suck him until the proverbial cows come home and never have to swallow so much as a drop of his spunk. The sin of wasting his seed in this specific way weighs heavily on his conscience. But all the other sins have found a home in him. His soul is blacker than tar, mostly because his mind is so fucked up. Let's face it, he's too inquisitive to be Catholic, but he was raised by a father who beat him regularly, who alternated between using a leather belt on his ass and bare fists on his face, and a mother who was a sister to the Catholic Church's top nun. It's left a seemingly permanent schism in his psyche. Four months ago he was a straight-A student at the university, studying to be an architect. Now he works as a ticket seller in a gay porno movie house over by the highway. It's run by the mob, and it's the only gay porno house left with a back room for sex.

There are a lot of things about Manny that don't make sense if you weren't raised Catholic, which I wasn't. Still, I've heard him babble on enough these last couple of months to put the pieces together. He started out a trusting little boy with a good heart, but dogma has doomed him to a destiny of sociopathic perversion. I try to tell him to get over it already, that this isn't Buffalo anymore, it's New York City. He can be whoever he wants to be. Sometimes he listens to me intently and makes love to me in the dark like he's starving for a sanctity he believes he can find in a woman's body. Other times the black cloud rolls over his face and the fist flies out, connecting with my cheekbone.

It was never my intention to save Manny from himself, just to lead him to the vast waters of the variety of human experience and let him drink. But the variety proved to be too much for his conscience. Sometimes without my knowing it, the things I'd want to do to him in bed would push him over the edge, and instead of succumbing to orgasm I'd end up dodging his fists. Lately I don't have the strength to wave so much as a white flag. I'm reduced to trying to read his mind and staying the hell out of his way.

I like it when Manny's at work. I like the fact that the movie house is open around the clock and that his shift in the little ticket-taker's booth is twelve hours long. It doesn't matter a bit to me that he's back to doing blow either. Even though it makes me spit each time I discover he's stolen hard-earned money from my wallet, I'd rather he spent all night in the horseshoe bar on East Seventh Street without me. Then he's more likely to skulk around the lower east side looking for more blow at 4 o'clock in the morning, increasing the risk of landing himself in the Tombs again. He hates the violence of the Tombs. He's come out of there sobbing. But having him locked in that mad monkey house is preferable to having his unpredictable rage lying next to me in bed.

I wish I could get him to give me back my key. I wish I could afford a locksmith to change the lock on my door. I'm going to find a way to get him out of here. I'm going to do it soon.

Ruby's band is back from their tour. She's trying to quit junk again, which means she's wanting to have sex with me. It's her pattern, and I've come to count on it. I love her so much it's scary.

I can't explain why I love Ruby. We have next to nothing in common. We don't seek the same highs. We don't like the same music. When we're lying together in bed we run out of things to say. I don't hang out in dyke bars like she does. I don't wear black leather. Even our tricks are from different worlds. I don't venture into the park after midnight to support a heroin habit. A cheap hand job in the shadows is not for me. My tricks are uptown men who shoot their spunk in broad daylight. Restaurateurs, entrepreneurs, and wealthy men whose emptiness is too complex for what can be gotten in ten minutes at twenty bucks a pop behind some bushes. Ruby wouldn't fare well in those uptown luxury apartments. She's not okay with being handcuffed. She doesn't own a pair of high heels. Holding on to a man's dick in the dark is the limit of what she can stomach. Pussy is where her heart is.

The first time I made out with Ruby, in a toilet stall at CBGB's, I didn't know she was on junk. I only knew she was a good kisser, which was why I'd followed her into the stall. We didn't do anything wild in there; we just kissed. We didn't unzip our jeans or pull up our T-shirts—nothing. But kissing Ruby was enough to make me fall in love. Her face up close to mine like that, her brown eyes closing, her dark hair brushing lightly against my face. Then the soft groans in her throat as our bodies rubbed against each other in that suggestive rhythm. I understand now why she seemed to be in slow motion. It wasn't some trance of Eros; it was the gold rushing through her veins.

I couldn't compete with the junk. It wasn't good enough for me. I wanted the whole girl. When I told Ruby that, we didn't kiss again for a year. I blew my money that year on the gypsies on Avenue C. Mostly on the youngest girl, the fourteen-year-old with the stray eye. I paid her to hold my hand in her lap, palm up, and tell me a pack of lies. I was too in love to leave anything to chance. I wanted my destiny spelled out for me. I wanted Ruby to come to her senses. She did, after three men in the park raped her one night. She called me collect from the pay phone in the emergency room at Beth Israel. She was ready to try it another way.

She moved back in with her mother in Queens. Six weeks later she showed up on East Twelfth Street, seeming doubtful, but her veins were clean.

If Ruby could find a way to keep off smack for good, there wouldn't be cracks in my world where vermin like Manny can wriggle in when I'm blind on bourbon and crying for myself. It's not that I kick Ruby out when she's shooting up; she just stops coming around. So I plug up the holes with whomever I can find. Now I have this dilemma. I want Ruby back in my bed. Nothing compares to her.

The first night Ruby and I made love it was the height of summer. Salsa music blaring from some Puerto Rican's boom box clashed with the tin calliope sounds of an ice cream truck parked under my open window. But in my double bed at the back of the flat the intrusions of the neighborhood faded. It was finally just Ruby and me. Both of us sober. When I saw her naked for the first time I felt elation, like how an exulting mother must feel as her eyes take in the body of her newborn for the first time, that unshakable faith in the existence of God. That's what it felt like

92

to see Ruby without her clothes on. How else can a mind account for something so perfect, so entrancing, so long desired? Her firm, upturned breasts with tiny, eager nipples. Her narrow waist, slim hips; the dot of her navel and the swirl of black hair that hinted at the mystery hiding under it all—at first, it made touching her a little daunting. But she lay down next to me and fervently kissed me. The force of passion coming from her slender body made the rest of it easy. I didn't worry about how to please her then. I knew intuitively what her body wanted. I could smell it coming off of her. Her nipple stiffening in my mouth needed more pressure. I twisted it lightly with my fingers instead. Tugging it, rolling it, pulling it insistently, while my mouth returned to her kisses. She moaned and her long legs parted. That's how simple it was.

I knew she would be wet between her legs. My fingers slid into her snug vagina, and her whole body responded, an invisible wave of arousal rolling over her that I could feel in the pressure of her kiss. The muscular walls of her slick hole clamped around my two probing fingers, hugging them tightly, making it too plain that the thick intrusive pricks of the pigs who'd raped her could only have entered her through sheer masculine determination. I knew how she had suffered. Struggling, succumbing, three times successively. It was hard to believe her body had withstood the repeated violation.

I shoved the pictures from my head. I centered my thoughts instead on the rhythm of her mound, how it urged my fingers to push in deeper. They did. Feeling my way, my fingers found the spot inside her that opened her completely, causing her thighs to spread wider; then she held herself spread, bearing down on my fingers as her slippery hole swelled around them.

I kissed my way down her ribs, down the flat expanse of her belly, following the wispy trail of hairs that led to the world between her legs. I wanted my mouth all over her down there. It was what I had dreamed of, ached for. At last, she was offering it to me, wide open and engorged.

Sometimes I think about how easy it was to make her come. Two fingers up her hole and my tongue on her clit, then the river of shooting sparks gushed through her. And because I loved her it made me happy to make her come, even though afterward we lay together entwined with nothing left to talk about. Ruby and I are always silent when we're finished making love.

With those wealthy tricks uptown it's more complicated. They need to discuss each detail. They practically draw you a map: the tit clamps here, the enema bag now, the length of rope like this, the gag last. The timing must be meticulous and the monologue rehearsed.

And with an uptight, paranoid guy like Manny it's even worse. There is no plan, no map—no discernible guide posts. Each gesture, every word, is a toss of the dice: Will it lead to a kiss or a bruised lip? I try not to lose sleep over it. If worse comes to worst, when Ruby arrives we'll shove the heavy bureau in front of the locked door. We'll go to my bed in the back of the flat, strip out of our clothes, and make love. Then I'll call the cops on Manny at last, when he's out in the hall shouting obscenities and slamming uselessly against the door.

the emperor of night

It happened that in olden times, in a land far, far away, an ancient people looked up lazily toward the approaching evening. The stars were not yet born, so the full-bellied moon was the sole celestial body in the nighttime sky. But on this evening, as twilight crept slowly toward the west, the startled people watched in awe as the sun reversed its setting and began to rise again. Along the far horizon of the sea it sprang up boldly and hid behind the full-bellied moon, and all the land fell into sudden night.

The Earth was remarkably still then, for this was a sacred darkness.

On the far side of the moon, under cover of the night, the mighty sun caressed the moon's fat belly with his eager fire, emptying his rays into her hidden crevices and filling her with his power until, it is said, she began to glow.

The glowing moon, unable to withstand her full-ness, surrendered to the penetrating flames of the mighty sun so completely that his flares burst through her swollen craters. And together, as the frightened people fled in all directions, the sun and moon exploded in a multitude of stars across the vast, unending sky.

The force of this explosion caused the land to shake and rock. It tugged at the swirling waves of the ocean waters, sending them leaping and curling upward, eddying in great swells. Until from the depths of the far-off South China Sea there emerged from the water a land of splendor, covered in a cloud of sea mist, whose center burned so gloriously that its proud inhabitants took no notice of the sunless sky. They knew that the sun now walked among them as a sacred man of fire.

This man of walking fire, created when the sun had burst across the heavens, came to be called, affectionately, the Emperor of Night.

The great emperor was loved by all his people. They basked in his bright fire and were nurtured by his light. Though the emperor taught his people the secret of making fire, none among the mere mortal subjects could ever build a fire whose flames outshone the emperor's. For in the emperor's heart there burned an eternal flame. A flame of longing; the seed of heaven itself.

In an effort to ease the daily burdens of his people, to give them a time of rest, when the sands had run through the hourglass twelve times, the emperor draped his regal body in a robe of black silk. Covering the essence of heaven, he shielded his land from the eternal burning flame of his heart while his people gently slept. And it was in this way that the emperor created night.

The emperor's grand palace was hidden on three sides by a shimmering, impenetrable cinnamon forest. Its courtyards were more hidden still behind the shade of mountain plum and wild pear trees, whose clustering blossoms the ladies of the palace had adorned with tiny silver chimes. The chimes tinkled in the delicate evening breezes and filled the nights with sounds of trembling music.

The palace itself had been intricately carved from mighty teaks and cedars. The sacred room where the emperor slept extended the length of the grand palace's fourth side, where it was buttressed against the power of the tossing sea by a huge wall of carved granite. So smooth it glistened, the granite wall formed a majestic lagoon of fresh seawater for the emperor alone. Here the cranes and herons, the crested kingfishers and loons nested in the protruding rocks amid the rarest night-blooming orchids and magnolia blossoms.

When the emperor adorned himself in his black silk robe and thus brought on the night, he retreated to his sacred solitude. Surrounded by the graceful calm of the nesting birds, visited only occasionally by harmless sea creatures who might swim under the great stone wall where the lagoon emptied into the waterway of the South China Sea.

The ladies of the palace were numerous, and each was as fair and sturdy as the emperor himself. Like him, their delicate faces were appointed with fine high cheekbones and dark almond-shaped eyes. In the daylight they wore their straight black hair in elaborate braids—sometimes adorned with tender peach blossoms or lilies of the valley. At night they let their hair hang free and exchanged their bright red robes for robes of black silk, so that each palace lady resembled the emperor in every respect save for what remained hidden beneath the folds of the austere black robes.

It was his custom that the emperor rarely slept, even though he'd created night, for great was the longing inside the eternal burning of his royal heart. He seldom passed the unending hours alone, sending for the various ladies of the palace to bring him companionship in the darkness.

None was to enter the emperor's sacred room, however. Each lady met him instead on the teakwood veranda opening onto the majestic lagoon. The veranda was gently illuminated by the tiny flickering flames of a hundred burning candles, each candle ensconced in an elaborately carved shade of ivory. The flickering flames produced tiny dancing shadows all along the granite wall: shadows in the shapes of flying dragons, miniature salamanders, or scattering wild geese. It was on this peaceful veranda that the emperor shared his pillow and mat with whichever lady he fancied. Being mindful, as he lifted her robe and led her through the many royal positions of tenderness and sharing, not to be wanton about the condition of his own robe, lest it loosen to reveal his heart and cause morning to arrive too quickly.

It is said that the emperor's eternal flame could be depleted only through the discharge of his seed into a woman who was not his bride. Though the burden of his eternally burning heart was great, the emperor was careful to preserve the power of his fire. The ladies of the palace were entrusted with a temper of restraint when arousing the emperor's pleasure. They were well-schooled in the art of pleasing him without bringing his royal seed to the point of expulsion.

The rare few among the palace ladies who took him past the brink of danger—who, knowing they could never be the emperor's bride, for the emperor's bride would not be mortal and would come in the form of a treasure offered up from the depths of the sea, still longed greedily to fill their barren wombs with the emperor's eternal fire— these few were punished swiftly and with severity. Taken by the palace guards to the hillside in the early morning, the offender was stripped bare of her protective robe and staked openly to an elevated cedar plank, her trembling legs forcibly raised and spread.

While the rest of the palace ladies were commanded to bear witness without lowering their eyes, the rare offender was subjected to the terrible Sixth Punishment, delivered by horse cock. Her wrenching screams were ignored until the mounting stallion's bulging shaft had completely rent her canal, making her no longer suitable for pleasuring the emperor.

Only then was the offender released and cast out from the palace walls. Only then were the palace ladies permitted to hide their faces in their sleeves.

It is said that on these bitter days, the emperor fasted alone and did penance in the royal chamber of his inner sanctum.

&

Every twenty-eight nights, however, a great thing happened. The emperor was permitted to expel his longing in the manner of an ancient ceremonial sacrifice.

Two ladies of the palace would be summoned to the teakwood veranda, where they assumed the Royal Position of the Gobbling Fishes. One lady lay atop the other in the posture of intercourse, their robes raised for the eyes of the emperor, their naked genitals rubbing together until their aroused labia swelled to resemble the mouths of gobbling fishes.

When they were close to orgasm, the emperor parted his robe and, kneeling between the spread thighs of the palace ladies, separated their swollen vulvas by easing his stiffening member between the engorged netherlips. The head of his royal shaft would pleasure their erect clitorises as it slipped in and out, until he himself was ready to discharge a burst of his eternal fire.

Then the emperor withdrew his member carefully and discharged himself into a golden chalice, held ready by a third lady of the palace.

This third lady was the most revered. Adorned in a ceremonial robe of luminescent silver, she walked side by side with the emperor as they carried the golden chalice into the calm lagoon together, to the spot where the oysters gathered. Here the emperor would select the most dazzling oysters. He would lovingly stroke his finger along the seam of their glistening shells and, with the tenderest of words, the emperor coaxed the oysters to reveal to him their secret pearls.

One by one the emperor would pluck the delicate pearls and drop them into the golden chalice that held his royal sperm.

After the pearls were selected and plucked and a ceremonial prayer recited, the golden chalice was emptied faithfully onto a sacred spot of jagged rock protruding from the waters of the quiet lagoon. For it was believed that in this way, the sea would be appeased and offer up to the emperor his long-awaited bride.

And here, at the sacred rock every twenty-eight nights, the emperor performed the supreme sacrifice: He removed the robe of luminescent silver from the lady of the palace, and while the two remaining ladies lay prone on the veranda and hid their faces obediently in their sleeves, the emperor prepared to teach his chosen lady the most secret of the royal positions.

"Soon you will learn the Position of Stealing Fire," the emperor announced tenderly. "In return, in gratitude for joining me in this supreme sacrifice, the emperor wishes to pleasure you."

The palace lady, now naked, her back steadied against the sacred rock, would assume the favored Royal Position of the Standing Heron, expecting to be pleasured by the emperor's stiff member, but on this ceremonial occasion the emperor would kneel in the salty seawater and place his mouth to the lady's tender netherlips.

A whimper of confusion and bliss would issue from the lady, as the sight of her emperor kneeling before her in the water, his royal mouth pleasuring her in an unexpected manner, was usually very troubling to a delicate lady of the palace. But the arousing pressure of the emperor's mouth exploring her tender secrets would cause the lady to surrender, until, within the tiny stiffening hood at the very tip of her mound, her pleasure peaked and she could endure no more of the sweetness. Her modesty then returned.

"Now I will teach you the Position of Stealing Fire," the emperor would instruct her solemnly as he rose from the water and parted the folds of his robe. "Come, kneel before me."

The naked lady trembled before her emperor and knelt in the water, respectfully lowering her eyes as he revealed himself. Taking her chin in his hand, he pressed his stiff member to the lady's quivering lips and commanded her quietly to open her mouth. So strange was the manner in which the emperor chose to pleasure himself that it was not uncommon for the chosen lady to lose her repose.

"Open your mouth," he would command her again, all the while keeping a mindful eye on the ladies lying prone on the veranda, lest they become too curious and lift their faces from their sleeves.

"You love your emperor, don't you?" he would entreat her. "You don't wish to see me lonely all my days?"

"No, my liege," came her heartfelt answer.

"Then you must help me to appease the sea or it will never offer up my bride."

Confused but ever faithful, the lady would be persuaded to part her reluctant lips and take the length of her emperor's thick shaft fully into her mouth. Then, as in the act of intercourse, he pleasured himself in her.

It was in this manner that the emperor discharged a second time, willingly sacrificing some of his fire, emptying it deep into the mouth of the chosen lady, a lady who was not his bride. The eagerness with which the emperor surrendered his fire and the helpless state to which he sank as it issued from his loins were the reasons this royal position was regarded as the most secret of all.

It was because this secret was so treasured by the palace—lest it be known among the ladies, who might seek to drain the emperor of his power—that the emperor, having sacrificed himself in her, regretfully closed his hands around the chosen lady's throat. As a sacrificial appeasement to the mighty sea, he held her pretty face beneath the salty water until she was thoroughly drowned.

The two remaining palace ladies were then permitted to lift their faces from their sleeves, and they assisted in silent ignorance as the emperor sent the lifeless body of the sacrificed third under the carved granite wall to be carried out to sea.

On those nights, the emperor slept. The following morning would dawn late on the land.

૨ລ

In the great emperor's thirty-second year, when he ached beyond reason to ease the burden of his burning heart, he donned his black robe and made it night. It was a sacred twenty-eighth night, and he was preparing to send for three ladies of the palace who would assume the Position of the Gobbling Fishes and hold the golden chalice ready to receive the royal seed, when suddenly the emperor noticed an eerie glow coming from the sacred spot on the jagged rock protruding from the majestic lagoon.

"At last," the emperor cried, but not too loudly, for he feared that the sound of his own voice might break some precarious spell.

Anxiously, he waded into the lagoon, carelessly forgetting to take care with his black silk robe.

"For many years I have been faithful," he exclaimed aloud. "I have spilled my royal seed every twenty-eighth night. I have offered the precious pearls and selected a palace lady for the supreme sacrifice. I have prayed that the eternal burning in my heart would come to peace. And now I see that the hour for rejoicing has indeed arrived."

The great emperor beheld that the eerie glow on the sacred rock issued from a membranous sac that contained a gestating female form. It was only a question of hours before the salty seawater would yield her, fully formed.

The emperor was so elated, so exalted in his joy that at long last the sea was responding to his tireless service and offering him up his bride, that he was tempted to hurry her progress by summoning more semen from within himself. Tempted to shower her with pearls. Even tempted to loosen his black robe and let the power of his fiery heart shine into her developing face and bring her more rapidly into being. But she was in a fragile stage. Patience was of the utmost importance.

The palace ladies, having not received the customary summons, had gathered in curiosity on the teakwood veranda, watching their emperor in awed silence as he stood waist-deep in the salty lagoon, his black robe soaking and his beautiful black hair blowing free in the gentle breeze.

More and more the sacred spot glowed before their eyes, slowly transforming the membranous sac into a discernible female form.

"She's come!" he announced at last, turning to address the palace ladies and weeping openly as the quickening wind showered his beautiful hair with falling petals, the clustered blossoms trembling on the trees and filling the air with the delicate music of the tiny silver chimes. "She has eyes!" he continued at last, gaining control of himself. "I've seen them glowing. She's opened her eyes!"

The ladies of the palace gasped and made haste in sending for the court magician to come and cut the delicate woman from the membranous sac and release her supple form to the Earth's atmosphere.

"It's happening very quickly now!" the emperor shouted, returning his attention to his creature. "She's moving rapidly along. We must *begin*. Where is my magician?"

The magician came at once in a cloud of jasmine smoke and a burst of iridescent light. Reciting a secret incantation that has long been forgotten by the palace ladies who witnessed the event, the magician set to work on the treasure from the sea. With his terrifyingly long, sharp fingernails, cultivated for just this occasion, he carefully tore the membranous sac free from the female creature.

With a sharp yelp, she cried as she encountered the open air then slid from the sac into the warm seawater.

It is said that when the emperor, to prevent her from slipping away from him and drifting out to sea, grabbed her in the water by one of her tender ankles and pulled her to him, she glowed all the more. At first it seemed that his robe had perhaps loosened, but this was not the case. The female creature contained a fire of her own.

The emperor lifted her carefully out of the water and into his arms. Through the viscous fluid that covered her, her golden hair glistened. She was round-eyed, round-bellied, and round-bottomed. She was so round and golden that the ladies of the palace were reminded of the fabled fat-bellied moon that had existed long ago. The moon that had waxed full as the mighty sun filled her to bursting, scattering them forever in a multitude of stars across the unending sky.

"You there!" the emperor pointed, as he set his treasured creature on the crowded veranda. "And you: Take her to the sacred chamber and ready her to be my bride. And you," he added, pointing to a third palace lady, "fetch my high priest from the inner sanctum and tell him of my great good fortune."

The ladies who had not been chosen bowed their heads in disappointment, stealing glances at the strange round-bottomed creature as she was escorted, on unsteady legs, to the sacred chamber.

"Disperse!" the emperor commanded.

In a flurry of black robes and flying hair, the ladies of the palace disappeared.

The emperor, masking his sudden terror with a dignified calm, beseeched of his court magician, "What becomes of me now?"

"What becomes of you?" the magician roared with delight. "What becomes of you? You administer the royal touch, you coax her lips to part. If she releases a pearl, she is indeed your bride. Then she will steal your fire and you will die." And with that, he disappeared in a cloud of jasmine smoke.

"*Steal* it?!" the emperor cried out to the vanishing smoke. "But I thought we were destined to *share* my fire, throughout eternity!"

"You will," a voice thundered on the scattering wind, "but the nature of everlasting love is first to surrender!"

ва

When the high priest was summoned from the inner sanctum and told of the great good fortune, he cautioned the palace ladies sternly, announcing that he would not be hurried.

"Preparing the emperor's bride—if she is, indeed, his bride— is a task that requires diligence and patience."

He entered the sacred room with a ceremonial demeanor. Like the emperor, the high priest was regal. He too wore a flowing robe of fine black silk. His face was appointed with the same high cheekbones, set off by piercing black, almond-shaped eyes.

If he felt at all aroused by the sight of the treasured creature, if his heartbeat quickened, he showed no signs of it. He approached the trembling female, whose watery round eyes blinked painfully in the candlelit chamber, and said quietly to her, "So you are the long-awaited treasure of semen and pearls, nourished on seawater and fire."

The female creature could not yet respond, though it seemed to those present that she understood his meaning.

"Tonight, my dear," he continued, "you will feel a burning sensation. This is natural, as you're adjusting to the surface of your own skin. Later, if the emperor can coax your lips to open and you release a pearl, then you are indeed his bride and will be forever. If you fail to produce a pearl, then it's simply not your time. You will dissolve once again into the sea, and we will resume our vigil. Come," he entreated her. "We will make you ready. We will start with the ceremonial ablution."

As the ladies readied the shallow basin, the high priest from the inner sanctum explained: "We don't want to shock the surface of her skin. We must proceed with precision and care. She has been nurtured on salty seawater until now. She will fight us if we don't introduce her to the purified water in increments."

The creature was helped to stand in the enameled basin and was held firmly at either arm by the palace ladies.

"I'll begin with your enchanting face," the high priest announced quietly. As he pressed the soaked sea sponge to the creature's delicate cheek, she resisted only slightly, for his touch was light. As he carefully washed the traces of the membranous sac from her unusual face, the high priest studied her thoughtfully. Though he'd never actually seen a round-eyed creature, he'd heard about them in fabled myths and legends, as he'd prepared his whole life for just this moment of readying the emperor's bride.

"That wasn't so bad," he encouraged her as he completed the cleansing of the creature's face and began on her pale shoulders. Her skin was still so new, so delicate, it was verily translucent, like gleaming pearls.

The priest dipped the sea sponge once again into the purified water and rinsed it lightly over the creature's arms. "You see," he directed the attention of the palace ladies, "how her skin is blanketed in golden hairs that weren't perceptible at first? She seems to be undergoing the final completion process right before our eyes."

The palace ladies marveled at the female with respectful awe.

"You see how the quality of her skin is changing?" he continued excitedly, bathing the beauty's arms. "How it is covered with downy hair? This is a very good sign."

When it seemed the female was steady enough on her feet, one of the palace ladies attended to the creature's hair. It was long and tangled and still slippery with the viscous fluid from the sac. The palace lady lathered the long golden strands with a mild soap normally reserved for bathing infants. Carelessly, however, the palace lady ascended a small stool and poured purified water over the top of the creature's head to rinse away the suds.

"No, no, no!" the high priest cried.

But it was too late. A terrible whimpering ensued that was of such a high pitch it pierced all their hearts and chilled their spines. The creature attempted to flee the basin, but the high priest grabbed her and steadied her back in the bowl.

"We'll try to be a little more careful," he assured her, glancing sternly at the palace ladies.

The creature blinked at him, seemingly terrified.

"That was probably the worst of it," he encouraged her again.

The lady culprit, in turn, stepped timidly from her stool and retreated quietly to a chair in the corner.

The high priest continued his steady, meticulous cleansing of the creature, washing her round breasts and her full, round belly. When he came to that delicate spot between the creature's legs, he carefully washed the membranous residue from her tightly curled golden hairs.

And then, to the surprise of all those present, the creature released her water, sending a stream of it in a great splash down into the basin. It was so sudden even the dignified high priest couldn't hide his surprise.

The two palace ladies glanced gleefully at each other, while the creature rapidly blinked her round eyes and smiled.

"You're pleased with yourself, is that it?" the high priest sighed.

The creature's eyes shone all the more.

"Well, as reluctant as I am to admit it, that was an extremely good sign. Come," he said, turning to the palace ladies, "we can't let her just stand in it. One of you empty this basin, and we'll attend to her feet."

&

At last the creature was washed and dried, her hair hanging in fluffy golden curls. The ladies helped her into an embroidered robe of crimson and, following the high priest, led her through an intricately carved passageway, deep into the sacred chamber where the great emperor anxiously waited.

No one but the high priest had ever entered this level of the emperor's sacred chamber. It was ablaze with flickering candles, and the palace ladies gazed in wonder at the splendid secret room, at the vibrant murals that lined its walls, depicting the distant mountains as they shimmered in an endless vista, rising beyond the mystical clouds.

The room itself was alive with flowers and smelled faintly of heaven. An aroma of dizzying fragrance scented the air.

Along one wall a towering waterfall trickled and splashed lightly over jagged layers of flat stones, adorned on either side by velvety moss and wild ferns. The water, which seemed to the palace ladies to originate somehow from the majestic lagoon, splashed endlessly into a deep but contained pool, where fat goldfish with billowy fins darted among the sunken rocks and underwater greenery.

The emperor himself was seated rather tentatively on a huge teakwood throne in the center of the chamber. It was set grandly on a raised platform of graduated marble, each level carved by hand to form ornate and opulent steps.

Beyond the throne, and mostly hidden from view by carved

ivory screens depicting the fable of the sun and moon in their coital embrace in heaven before they burst into the multitude of stars, stood the royal bed. From where they stood the ladies could see a beautiful lace netting, suspended from a delicate fixture in the ceiling, draped over the royal resting place like a heavenly veil. The palace ladies recognized this exquisite lace as the type made by the ancient ladies of the distant palisades, the cliff-dwelling ancients who lived so high in the peaks that even in the scorching days of mid-summer they could not be reached without first traversing deep gorges of ice and snow for many days.

When the great emperor realized the palace ladies were too curious for his comfort, he dispersed them. His high priest, though, remained behind.

"Tell me," the emperor beseeched him. "How do I live through this night? If she won't produce a pearl, she will dissolve into salty water, and I will die from the pain of losing her. If she does produce a pearl, I am told she will steal my fire. Either way, I will die."

The high priest chose his words carefully. "There is much I do not know. I only know we have prepared for this throughout our entire existence. If the time has not yet come for her to be your bride—and let me add that the signs do not seem to point to this outcome—rest assured she will come again, at a more propitious time. For that is the nature of all that exists. That is the ebb and flow of life, and that is the law of the sea. If, however, her time has come and she is ready to accept your fire, look on it as a release. You will not die, not in the mortal sense. You will transmogrify into something grander, for you are an energy that will never end."

The emperor tried to take comfort in the high priest's words, but he could not overlook the hint of sorrow creeping into the high priest's face.

"I've been lonely far too *long*," the emperor began. But then he saw that mere words were useless in the face of destiny, and so he bid his high priest to take leave of the sacred chamber.

໖

The emperor parted the lace netting and helped his bride onto the conjugal bed. It was a fine, large bed of carved cedar and padded with a thick mat of embroidered silk over a layer of down. The emperor could not help but marvel at his creature. Her fine limbs and well-appointed face made her seem quite human, but her curling tresses and translucent skin were much softer than anything he'd known.

He propped her tender back against a pile of soft pillows and then climbed onto the bed himself. He knelt next to her and studied the perfect roundness of her form. Her eyes, in particular, intrigued him; they seemed to brim with understanding. She regarded him with a curious, penetrating gaze.

He loosened her crimson robe and examined her more closely. Such full breasts and the roundest belly—like nothing he had ever seen. She seemed an odd mixture of virginity and fecundity.

"You look like you're going to have a child," he whispered to her playfully.

Of course she said nothing in reply, as she had not yet learned to speak.

"You look soft enough to sleep on," he continued, then reached out to stroke her belly. He thought increasingly of lying on top of her, of removing his robe completely, to feel for the first time in his life what it might be like to couple completely with a naked female.

The more he imagined himself coupling with her, the more he stroked her fat belly, until he realized she was entranced by his touch and beginning to respond.

Her legs parted to reveal her netherlips, covered in tiny golden curls. These were the lips that would part completely and produce the treasured pearl if she was in her season.

The emperor, intrigued but tentative, pushed aside her robe completely. Braving what he did not know, he resolved to examine her tender secrets.

Very human-like, he thought at first. He caressed the tip of her mound to see if she would respond.

Respond she did, as the emperor had never witnessed.

She moaned sweetly and offered her secret parts to him completely. She knew no modesty. The more he stroked her there, the more aroused she got. Her netherlips became engorged, separating more like the petals of orchids than like any human female sex. And the tip of her mound seemed to please her so thoroughly that the emperor lost himself in caressing her there.

She undulated and moaned so, and her lips grew so enticingly ripe, that he couldn't help but want to pleasure her there completely. He pressed his mouth to her tender flesh and was overwhelmed by his own excitement. Caught up in her cries and whimpers, and the strange rhythms that flowed from her, the emperor was no longer aware of the time, of whether he should make it day or night. Paying no mind to the condition of his robe, he set aside the cares of his people. So entranced was he by her delight, all his senses focused on pleasuring his creature.

The more fervently his mouth explored her, the more eager were her cries. The more her cries entranced him, the more fervently he desired to please her, unaware that the strange rhythms swelling in her were setting his destiny in motion.

In ignorance, he licked and sucked at her delicate petals, his tongue caressing every tender fold, until the urges of his pounding manhood overtook him. He knew his moment had arrived. He would lay on top of her, with no fear of dying, and receive the blessings of heaven.

The emperor tossed aside his robe. His creature glowed all the more profoundly in the presence of his fiery heart.

He raised her legs to mount her, to guide his stiff member into the folds of her tender flower, when he observed, with shock and awe, a tiny, perfect pearl push through her sacred opening!

The emperor's consternation was great. "No," he cried, at the same time feeling elated that she was, indeed, his bride—his for eternity—that she would not dissolve into seawater.

Still the sight of the pearl chilled him. *"How will you steal my fire?"* he demanded. *"How is it that I will die?"*

But the creature only stared at him, round-eyed, and smiled. Pleased with her pearl, delighted with what her aroused body had created for him.

The emperor picked up the pearl and examined it closely. He knew what was expected of him. He was to send for his high priest and offer the pearl to the mighty sea with a prayer of gratitude and thanksgiving.

"And then what?" he said quietly, searching the face of his bride.

The shaken emperor clutched the tiny pearl tightly in his fist, knowing that it represented his doom. "If only it could have remained inside!"

He gathered his robe around him and prepared to send for his high priest. "If only it could have remained inside," he repeated morosely.

And it was at this moment, it is said, that the great Emperor of Night resolved to betray the will of heaven.

❧

"Drink this," the emperor urged his bride.

He held the wine chalice to her lips, having placed the sacred pearl on her trusting tongue.

"It's wine from the Azure Mountain. It will help the pearl slide down."

The emperor's bride drank the wine and found it quite pleasing, holding out her empty goblet for more.

"No," the emperor replied. "Now is the time for tenderness and sharing."

❧

Outside the palace walls the emperor's weary subjects rose, groggy and overly tired, surprised to discover daylight had arrived so quickly. They dragged their heavy plows through the fields, milked their startled cows, and poked at the sleeping sheep to herd them out to the meadows. It wasn't long, though, before news of the arrival of the emperor's bride reached even the farthest hamlets. With knowing sighs, the weary people retreated back to their bedchambers, with the realization that it was, in fact, the middle of the night.

❧

The robe of crimson lay in a gentle heap atop the robe of black silk on the floor of the emperor's sacred chamber. The fine lace netting draped over the conjugal bed as if it were indeed a veil from heaven, protecting the lovers from the cares of the outside world.

Though the emperor knew many royal positions for tenderness and sharing, he soon found he was most content when merely lying atop his bride. For in this way, he discovered—as many lovers have discovered since the beginning of time—he could lie with his bride filling his strong arms while their secret parts entwined in a coital union. Their mouths could exchange deep kisses while the emperor ran his fingers through her soft, golden hair. But what thrilled the emperor most of all was that while they assumed this entwining embrace—belly to belly, mouth against mouth, his stiff member penetrating deep into her secret flower as her legs wrapped around his waist—the soft, round breasts of his bride pressed full against the emperor's fiery heart. How long had he waited for a night like this to ease his torment? The emperor no longer knew. The years of loneliness, of yearning in his loins, seemed as remote now as if they had never been part of his experience.

Many times the sands slipped through the hourglass that night, and many times the emperor discharged his fiery seed into the flower of his eagerly responsive bride. The more he shared his fire with her, the more his creature seemed to glow. The emperor was delighted with the passion of his manhood, how it never seemed to wane. No sooner would he discharge his royal seed in her than his member would grow thick and he would penetrate her flower again.

So lost in each other's arms were they, so entranced with all their senses, the emperor did not notice the high priest enter the sacred chamber until he was readily perceived to be standing just beyond the heavenly veil.

Angered by the intrusion, and protective of the modesty of his bride, the emperor displayed a temper previously unknown to the high priest.

"Your majesty will forgive me, I'm sure," he apologized, "but there's the matter of the sacred pearl..."

The emperor, stricken by a raw sensation of guilt over having induced his innocent bride to betray heaven with him and swallow the sacred pearl, answered haltingly, "What about it?"

"Your majesty, the sands have slipped through the hourglass twenty-four times; surely she has released a pearl by now."

"Of course she's released a pearl! She's my bride, mine for eternity."

"Yes, your majesty, but—"

"But *what?!*"

"You never sent for me. We must offer the pearl back to the sea as a gesture of gratitude and thanksgiving."

The emperor was more guilt-stricken still. "I've seen to the matter already," he declared.

The high priest tried hard to hide his feelings of alarm.

"I told you, the matter's been seen to!" the emperor insisted. "I saw no reason to part from my bride for even a moment longer than was necessary, so I tossed the pearl into the lagoon myself and gave a prayer of thanks. I assure you, it was heartfelt. No doubt, your grace will understand my sense of *urgency.*"

The high priest could not hide his dismay. Still, he approached his emperor with caution. "I dare say, that's not the manner in which these things were expected to be done, but I suppose what matters is that the ritual was carried out, so that heaven and the mighty sea will be appeased."

The emperor replied hotly, "They're appeased."

"I beg your majesty to suffer me just a moment longer."

"What is it?!" the emperor shouted.

"It's the matter of your people, your majesty. They tire from the constant day. Might you consider donning your robe for a time, if only for the sake of your people?"

"I have lived my whole life for the sake of my people. Surely they can grant me a little patience in this instance!"

And that was all the emperor deigned to offer on the subject.

❧

Finally, it came to pass that the emperor grew tired. He slipped into his robe and lay with his head on a pillow next to his bride and closed his weary eyes. But it seemed his eyes had only been closed a moment when he felt his member stiffen and again become thick.

He opened his eyes in time to see his beautiful bride climb astride him, burying his protruding shaft deep within her hot flower.

And, indeed, it was hot. It was so hot and so deep that the emperor wished to lose himself completely in her warmth, be absorbed into her body and drift to a never-ending sleep. His eyes closed at last, filled with the vision of her nakedness, her full breasts gently sloping down, and her round golden belly undulating enticingly as she pleasured herself on his royal member.

❧

When the emperor awoke he feared he was dying. He did not know how long he had slept, but he sensed it had been an inordinately long time.

He was chilled to the bone. He reached down to the floor for a coverlet, but it did little to warm him.

His bride was awake and lying cheerfully beside him. A heat came from her radiant glow that beckoned the emperor close. He took her in his arms and kissed her and, without even knowing it, drifted back into a deep sleep.

૪☙

"Your majesty will forgive the intrusion."

It was the high priest again, shaking the emperor gently by the sleeve of his black silk robe.

"Your majesty, wake up."

"Yes, what is it?" The emperor tried to focus on the high priest, but his brain longed for more sleep.

"Your majesty, we have a crisis. The land has been stuck in what can best be described as a gray half-twilight for many days. The people are growing restless and cold. They threaten to chop down the entire forest for fire."

The emperor went to great lengths to understand the high priest's words, but all he really understood was the direness of his tone.

"Surely the blissful sleep after the wedding night has gone on long enough," the high priest entreated him. "The robe, your highness. Your people could use some sun."

"Fine," the emperor managed to reply, and with a tremendous physical effort he stripped away his black robe and fell dead asleep.

In a moment the troubled high priest had returned. "Your majesty, it didn't help. The gray twilight remains."

The emperor's powerful will roused him from his deep need for sleep. He pulled his bride to him, as he suffered now from an extreme chill, but she was so fiery hot, he sprang away from her.

"Your majesty! What is it?" The high priest made no pretense to mask his alarm. "You look so ashen and pale."

"It's her!" he cried, fearing for the wellness of his bride. "She positively burns with fever!"

The emperor's bride lay happily among the royal pillows.

"She seems quite well to me. She's glowing and rounder than ever."

"No," the emperor sputtered wearily. "She's on fire. Touch her."

The high priest laid his hand on the bride's arm then pulled it sharply away as if he had been burned. "You're right! She burns with fever. Yet you are the one who looks ill."

"I've made a grave error in judgment, your grace," the emperor struggled to confess. "I tried to prolong my happiness and still I am dying. You see how she steals my fire? Only now she will perish too; my fire is consuming her."

The high priest urged the emperor to explain.

"The pearl," he managed to say. "I cheated heaven. I made her swallow the sacred pearl. I tried to hide from my fate by making her consume the product of our passion. I fear now that it is burning her alive."

The high priest ran from the chamber to summon the nearest palace ladies. "You must fetch the magician. There's been a tragic accident. The emperor and his bride are quite ill."

Amid the great weeping and hysteria of the palace ladies, the emperor and his bride were draped in ceremonial robes and gingerly transported to the teakwood veranda, where they were placed on a sacred mat.

The magician arrived in a burst of iridescent light and a cloud of jasmine smoke.

When it was revealed to the magician how the emperor had attempted to betray the will of heaven, he demanded that the court disperse, even the high priest, and gather in the inner sanctum to pray for the emperor's soul.

When the magician was alone with the emperor and his bride, he gently shook the emperor, who had once again drifted into a deep sleep.

"You have been a fool," the magician declared quietly. "You had all that heaven allowed and still you wanted more."

"I know," the emperor confided. "I've seen my mistakes played out behind my eyes in quite vivid and remorseful dreams. I have an unbearable burden in my heart. I no longer mind that I am dying, but I have sealed the fate of my innocent bride, and who will look after my people when I am gone? See how the stars are forever approaching from the east, yet they never arrive? It is not day, it is not night; will my people be forever trapped in this twilight? And my poor bride. She burns with enough fire to light an empire, yet she cannot shine and save my kingdom."

"I know what must be done," the magician replied, seemingly unmoved by the emperor's plight. "How, may I ask, is the condition of your heart? Have you left anything undone? Have you said your prayers for your people?"

The emperor nodded gravely. "But what about my bride? I will never be ready to tell her goodbye."

"Your majesty," the magician scolded him, "you are such a foolish man! Your destiny has never been anything but that: your destiny. I told you your love was ordained by fate to last throughout eternity, but love requires you first to surrender. Nothing you do can exert your will over the will of heaven. All you've managed to create in the meantime is human misery and delay."

The emperor's eyes edged with tears. He summoned great strength within himself, braved his creature's hot fire, kissed her tender mouth one last time, and surrendered to the will of heaven.

He tried to contain his tears as he watched his court magician conjure an incantation over his blissfully ignorant bride. And then, with not even a moment for him to prepare, a mighty gale of wind swept across the veranda, and the emperor's treasured creature shot up to the sky as a crackling ball of fire.

Day dawned instantly on the land, and all that was left behind for the emperor to cling to was his creature's sacred pearl. The treasure their joy had created had withstood the powerful fire.

It is said that in his profound grief the emperor swallowed his creature's pearl. And as the magician disappeared in a cloud of jasmine smoke and a gentle breeze tinkled the tiny silver chimes in the tender plum blossoms, the emperor wept bitter tears and did not stop weeping, even after the sands had slipped through the hourglass twelve more times.

And it is further said that so great was the emperor's remorse, he could no longer provide night for his tired people, who toiled in constant daylight. So bitter were his tears, he finally dissolved into salty water that trickled down into the majestic lagoon and was carried out to sea.

It was then that the mighty waves leaped and swirled and tossed a sacred glowing pearl far into the western sky, at last bringing on the gentle evening. And it was this sacred pearl, which we've come to call our moon, that was loved in ancient times by a tender, tired people who came to call it, affectionately, the Emperor of Night.

i like boys

I like boys who look young, without a lot of body hair. Boys who maybe just dropped out of college. Boys who wish they knew a lot but know they haven't got a clue. Boys who feel overwhelmed by me because I'm so much older.

I like boys who consider themselves straight but who, after spending a long time talking with me in my bed in the dark, eventually admit that they might be bisexual, that sometimes they've even worried that they're actually gay.

I love to hear stories a boy has never told another living soul. Like the one about the stretch of yard behind his parents' house, hidden from the world, where he'd lowered his jeans and let his buddy get between his legs and suck his dick. The story usually involves the boy's surprise over having gotten "so hard, so fast" and his emotional mixture of desire and loathing as he'd watched his own dick growing stiffer as it moved in and out of his buddy's mouth. Usually there's a part about the buddy having seemed "too eager"—which unnerves the boy still, in his telling of the secret tryst—an eagerness that had compelled the boy to grab onto his buddy's head and pump into his mouth hard, until the jism shot out with such uncontrollable force that his buddy had had to hold tight to the boy's bare thighs in an effort to keep his balance.

You can't beat hearing a story like that—it's a sign that a boy trusts you.

I like it when a boy trusts me; it means we're likely to go places together. I don't mean to cafés or bars or nightclubs. I'm talking about those less tangible places, which usually involve taking all our clothes off and not leaving the apartment for a few days. Where take-out food deliveries are our only meals and even the wine is ordered in.

I like going places with a boy that involve changing into different outfits and different shoes and then leaving them strewn all over the apartment. And wearing down my favorite tube of lipstick because it keeps smudging off on the wineglass, the cigarette filters, the slightly rough unshaved face, and the boy's thick, stiff cock. Or sometimes the lipstick smudges off onto the pillowcase if I happen to have my face buried there, biting on the pillow because I'm getting that thick cock stuffed into me hard from behind.

That's when the boy seems most like a man, though. That's when the subtle aroma of the wine—as you take a break from fucking and pour it into the wineglasses, which are just in reach on the night table—that aroma only serves to remind you of how elusively time passes. It helps if it's twilight and through the open window you can see the lights coming on through the trees across the Hudson River.

ò&

I like boys who watch me very intently as I start to tie them up. They're not in a hurry to protest, but they're young enough to be unsure of how far I'm likely to go. I like when a boy feels like he doesn't have to be in control, though. Like, maybe I've tied him down spread-eagle to the bed and he's watching intently as I kneel between his spread legs. Then I slide his erect cock in and out of my lipsticked mouth. When he feels my finger slip up his ass, he doesn't complain.

Or how a boy surrenders when you slip the blindfold over his beautiful eyes? I like that, blindfolding a boy who's tied down. I can plant my soaking pussy right on his mouth then and he acts like he's never wanted a pussy more in all his life. He devours my swollen lips with a lot of passion, as if not having a choice in the matter is what's really turning him on.

Sometimes it's fun to turn around then. To keep my pussy planted on his mouth but lean down and let my tongue lick lightly at his piss slit. Let it run up and down his aching shaft, maybe lick determinedly at the spot just under the swollen crown—or maybe down under his balls—but not take his whole dick in my mouth again for a while.

A boy can get really excitable when my mouth is doing stuff like that. He'll moan distractedly, or go at my clit with such enthusiasm that I start wondering how he can even breathe.

But here's what I really like: a boy who isn't afraid to show me his asshole, who might even like to lie belly-down and spread his legs for me while I admire him. I like it best if he doesn't want to be tied then, because it indicates to me that he's really *wanting* it. I like it when a boy is really wanting it—the anilingus part. I do that first. I try to be really thorough and patient with a rim job. I push his cheeks apart and hold them spread while my tongue licks slowly at his hole, or around his hole, or up and down his crack, because it really helps a boy relax. And a boy needs to feel relaxed. He needs to feel he can trust me, because I'm going to strap on a greased-up silicone tool and slide it up his ass and he knows it. Sometimes he's even been the one to ask for it.

And if he's liking it enough, if he's into it and his hole is opening up easily for me, I'll probably fuck him hard. Hold onto his arched ass while I fuck him and tell him how beautiful he looks, how incredible his ass is as it takes the tool in deep. Maybe I'll even have him pull his knees up under himself so he can jerk off while he's getting reamed. And then the noises he'll start to make—God, the grunting. I love to listen to those lusty sounds a boy getting fucked is likely to make.

But it won't happen at all if a boy's not willing to turn over for me. Which doesn't mean I don't like boys who won't turn over.

I even like those boys who like it best when I'm flat on my back, who hike my long legs up over their shoulders and keep my wrists pinned down to the mattress with their large, substantial hands. Who shove their dicks into me deep, over and over— maybe getting in too deep. Who seem to like the fact that I'm grunting like an animal, even while my mouth is being kissed— devoured, almost; his tongue shoving in and filling my mouth while I whimper.

I like a boy who knows enough to keep fucking me even if it sounds like I'm in pain.

&

I like when a boy lights up a cigarette in the dark—after we've finished fucking, maybe, and there's a jism-filled condom lying somewhere on the bed but no one wants to turn on the light yet and find it. So we lie there instead, naked and entwined, and share a cigarette. Pass it back and forth, even though we've heard all about how smoking is no good for us.

I like a worn-out boy to lay his head against my bare breasts in the tangle of sheets and pillows while I hold him in the crook of my arm and we share that cigarette in bed. There's something about that fiery glow as we drag on the cigarette in the darkness; it makes confessions seem simple. Boys will tell you the oddest things if the room's really dark and they're sure no one but you can hear them. I'm not big on confiding, myself, but I love to listen to a boy's dreams.

i'm sorry

My mother was thirteen years old that Friday when I was born, back in the summer of 1960, in a county home for unwed mothers. And in keeping with the pathos of the situation, Brenda Lee's "I'm Sorry" was a number 1 Billboard smash hit on Top 40 radio stations nationwide. I was unceremoniously dragged, with the use of forceps clamped over my eyes, out of my young mother's vagina while teenage girls all over America commiserated with the plight of poor Brenda Lee.

My mother was unrealistic about a lot of things, I guess, especially regarding her plans for me—her newborn, her little treasure. She was packing my meager belongings, which consisted of some cloth diapers and a cotton blanket, in preparation for our leaving the county home at last and returning to her real bed, in her little room in a small house in a small southern Ohio town, when my grandpa came in and gave her the news. The folks from the private adoption agency that he'd called behind her back had come to collect the baby, me.

My mother had been under the naive impression for nine long months that the baby growing in her ever-expanding womb was hers. The same fetus that had incited other kids at Lincoln Junior High School to call her "whore" and that was now a squalling, beet-red, warm-blooded infant gift from God, needing her nipple. The forced separation devastated her. She embarked almost immediately on a new illegitimate pregnancy that brought her first a hasty marriage and then a lifelong cocktail hour in one hillbilly bar after another. She learned the hard way that no number of pregnancies could replace the baby they'd taken away. Even though I was barely cognizant back then, I don't think I was too wild about the separation either. I spent the next twenty-five years wishing achingly on a lot of stars, with a huge gaping void in my soul. My nightly prayers were filled with pleas like *God, can I please have my real mother back?*

She was thirty-eight years old when I finally found her. She normally worked as a barmaid and lived off the Appalachian highway in some holler with a truck driver. But the day my letter arrived in her mailbox, she was just getting out of a brief stint in jail.

I wasn't the person she most wanted to think about right then. She tossed my letter onto the kitchen counter and lit a cigarette. The enclosed baby pictures had been taken twenty-five years earlier by a somewhat affluent married couple up north.

It was Decoration Day when she finally agreed to meet me. Decoration Day is what Southerners call Memorial Day—when you go out to the graveyard and place flowers on the tombstones of soldiers you knew who died in a war, then place flowers on the tombstones of your other deceased loved ones, as long as you're out there.

She agreed to meet me in neutral territory: the tiny, spotless kitchen of my Aunt Kate.

My mother came in the kitchen door that afternoon, after twenty-five years of being separated from her baby, followed by one of the most magnetically attractive girls I'd ever seen. She was almost as tall as I was, but she was much more solidly built. She had large, muscular arms and thick, sturdy legs. She was fairly dark-complexioned, with dark brown hair, coal-black eyes, and wide, high cheekbones—the result of being born half Shawnee. I was smitten with her, instantly in love. *Here's my dream lover,* I thought. *What is she doing hanging out with my mom?*

I had a predilection back then for getting spanked by large women. I took one look at that dark-haired girl's massive arms and thought, *This is going to be great. Somehow I have to get my fanny over that girl's considerable knee.*

I was already deep into the quivering-clit stage of a fantasy that involved having my jeans and underpants around my thighs and lying across this girl's lap when my Aunt Kate introduced me to my younger half sister, Rae Anne. She'd been eighteen for three whole weeks already, I was told, and was due to graduate high school the following weekend. I'd come back into my mother's fold just in time to witness an unusual family occurrence: a high school graduation. Most of the family were dropouts.

My newfound mother was emotionally distant, offering me no more than a quick hug when she said hello, but spirits in general were running high. With me back in her life, my mother would soon be able to claim *two* daughters that had graduated high school.

Rae Anne and I sat alone together out on our aunt's driveway in a couple of folding aluminum patio chairs. Conversation between us was stilted and awkward. I stared at her a lot—I was in awe, having always wanted a sister. But she made very little eye contact with me in return, her eyes darting away nervously whenever she'd try to steal a glance at me and then find I was still staring.

"So what kinds of things do you like to do?" I asked, in a feeble attempt to get her talking as quickly as possible about her sexual experiences.

"Oh, I like to play basketball, fix cars, motorcycles, that kind of thing."

Thank you, God, I thought, *she's a dyke—but I wonder if she knows it yet?*

"Mom says you're a singer in New York City."

"Yeah," I replied. "I sing country music in these shitty bars, and I wait tables during the day. I was married to a Chinese man for a little while, but we're separated now because he'd rather be gay and I'm fooling around with a woman."

There, I thought, *direct, to the point. Check out that astonished expression on her face.*

"Really?" she asked, her voice hushed. The back screen door was open and the rest of my newfound family was still sitting close by in the kitchen, chatting over coffee and my Aunt Kate's cherry pie. "You sleep with girls?"

"Uh-huh," I said, studying her expression. *Come to me, baby, tell me things.*

"Really? For real?"

"Yes."

She was fidgeting uneasily in her aluminum patio chair. She leaned closer to me and confided, "I'm gay. But I haven't told Mom."

Hallelujah, I thought, *she knows.* "Are you planning on telling her?"

"No, man, I couldn't tell her that—she'd freak."

I scooted my chair closer to hers and said, "She didn't freak when I told her about me."

"You told Mom you sleep with *girls?*"

"Uh-huh."

"And she didn't freak?"

"No. I told her all kinds of things. She knows all about me."

&

Later that night, when everyone had gone home, I lay alone in a king-size bed. My Aunt Kate and Uncle Paul had graciously moved into their tiny guest room so that I could enjoy the luxury of their sizable bed. I felt like a treasured guest who had come a long way in a treacherous night. I'd quickly discovered that most of my mother's relations felt guilty over my grandfather's decision to cast me out to perfect strangers. They all bent over backward to make me feel comfortable, in a genuine display of joy over the fact that I was finally back with my mother. Maybe now all the guilty feelings could be buried.

Alone in the unfamiliar bedroom, my thoughts drifted not to my long-sought mother or the emotionally distant stance she'd taken toward me but to my new half sister.

"Is there anything you want for your graduation that you don't want Mom to know about?" I'd asked her before she got in the car to go home.

Rae Anne had smiled. "A fifth of gin?"

"Gin it is," I'd promised her. "Just don't drink and drive."

What an amazing turn my life had taken. I was going to be present at my sister's graduation with a secret bottle of gin. My mother was going to bake a cake, and the trucker she lived with was pulling out the stops and planning to buy beer and whiskey and have food brought in for everybody. I was even going to get to meet my half brother, who'd be coming in from the neighboring town, where he lived in a trailer with his dad.

He was the black sheep of the family, my half brother. Another high school dropout, with a volatile temper. A half-Shawnee alcoholic who was always in jail. It felt great to finally be in a family dynamic where I was perceived to be the golden child who had done great things: I was a singer in New York City who'd married a man from far-off China. The family who had raised me held a decidedly different opinion of me. After all, I'd married a known faggot—who was Chinese, of all things; I slept around with girls, some of them junkies, most of them musicians; and I wasted my life singing in bars.

Suddenly I was very pleased with my exotic lifestyle, and I couldn't wait to spend more time with my sister, regaling her with tales of what it was like to hang out in queer bars and openly bring girls home to fuck.

"I've only been with a couple women," she'd said quietly. "My gym teacher and then her daughter, and one other girl. But I know that's what I want, I want to be with women. I don't care what people think."

But she still had to be extremely careful. Doing it in her car at night, after pulling off some back road and parking under the

127

cover of trees. I remembered what *that* was like—being young and having to hide it. Fucking boys was one thing. You definitely didn't want your parents to catch you doing that. But fucking a girl? It would have been the end of the world.

As I lay alone in that big bed, I began to wonder what kinds of things my sister was doing to girls in her car. I wondered if Rae Anne was anything like me—if she hungered for the things I hungered for, or had a taste for the things I liked. Then I started to wonder what her body looked like when she got completely aroused. When she was out of her clothes, spreading her legs in the backseat. What did her pussy look like to some girl whose face was coming up close to it? What would the lips look like when some girl's fingers were spreading her open, when some girl's mouth was finding her swelling clit—did my sister's pussy look anything like mine? And if so, did that mean I looked like my mom?

I had my fingers between my legs by then, masturbating as quietly as possible in my aunt and uncle's bed while the pictures filled my mind. The images blossomed with remarkable clarity, and my entire body succumbed to the sensitivity of my clit. I could see my sister perfectly in the backseat of that car, because I was in there with her; it was my own face disappearing between her legs as my tongue found her swelling clitoris and made her moan. I just wanted to make her happy; it pleased me to hear her guttural groans and cries. It would be like playing together—only now we were grown and we had special secret games to play in the backseat of her car. We'd missed those years of being little together, of being confidantes and pals. Of jumping around in our PJs on a Saturday morning until our mother lost her patience—listening to all that noise—and came in to spank *somebody,* but which little naughty girl would it be?

This time I was hoping it would be Rae Anne. I'd like to see my little sister get spanked by my mom. *There she goes,* I thought, *over my mother's knee. Down come her little pajama bottoms and then spank spank spank, until her tiny naked tushy is fiery-red.* I'd spent too many years wearing out my own getting-spanked fantasies. I didn't need to see them anymore. I'd summoned them so many times over the years that they'd worn a dull path through my mind's eye and couldn't ignite my clitoris anymore. Fantasies of being alone with my secret mother. My special gift-from-God mother, who hadn't left me behind, who hadn't given me up. Who, in fact, loved me so much that she had to do what was best for me: teach me a lesson and take me over her knee. *Spank spank spank.* Until the fantasies progressed to real life, to real women that I met in bars. Women who agreed to take me over their knees but who didn't stop there. Who made me put on those frilly white ankle socks. Who insisted my pussy be shaved smooth. Women who gagged me with pink bandannas, threw me onto the bed, and tied my wrists too tightly. Who went too far, who took me out to the edge, making me come after they inserted the douche nozzle in my ass when my ankles were tied somewhere up over my head. And then the warm water streamed steadily into my rectum, filled me up, while a hand slapped my ass *harder harder harder* and a kind but firm voice warned me to hold the water in.

❧

The night before my sister graduated from high school, my mother and her boyfriend took Rae Anne and me out to a hillbilly bar for a seemingly endless amount of malt liquor. My sister was still too young to drink legally in a bar, but she wasn't disappointed. She had a brand-new bottle of gin in the backseat of her car. I, on the other hand, was more than old enough to drink, but I never drank malt liquor. The sheer number of drinks being placed in front of me that night was making me queasy. But my mother was on a roll.

"She's the baby that mattered, you know," she drunkenly informed my little sister. "She was more important than the rest of you." (I had yet another half sister that I would meet the next day at the graduation, along with my grandpa, the man who had sealed my fate that summer day in 1960.)

When at last I reached my limit, my sister and I left the bar, got into her car, and went for a drive along the back roads.

"You can't imagine what it was like, Rae Anne, growing up alone. To never feel like you fit in with the people around you because they all look like one another and you don't look like any of them. It was lonely. I didn't know you even existed, but I sure missed Mom, every day of my life."

"It's good you came home," Rae Anne said. "It's been good for Mom too. I can see a difference in her already. You're her victory over Grandpa, you know."

We were driving into total darkness. There were no street-lights, no houses, not even a gas station. But my sister knew her way around those back roads. We came to a railroad crossing, and she veered off to a clearing and parked the car.

I was drunk enough on malt liquor to feel unabashedly aroused. We were safe under cover of darkness, my sister and I, miles away from anyone we knew. Maybe now would be a good time to tell her about my theory, about how incest couldn't be wrong if it was between two consenting adults who couldn't possibly conceive an inbred accident. Maybe now would be a good time to regale her with stories of how liberating it feels to bring a girl home and fuck openly, to not have to hide in a cramped car while trying to cram your eager face between a girl's spread legs. *That's it,* I thought, *start talking dirty, that's how the juices start churning—from the pictures you plant in someone's head.*

So I started with the dirty talk and I was making Rae Anne laugh. Uneasily at first, but then she joined in with her own dirty stories, stories about eating pussy and how turned-on she got looking between a girl's legs.

Then I unbuttoned my shirt, a faded denim work shirt. I wasn't wearing a bra.

"Do your tits look like mine?" I asked quietly, pinching my nipples a little so they'd perk up and get stiff. "Huh, do your tits look like these?"

Even though it was dark in the car I could feel my sister staring hard at me, trying to see.

"Do you think we're alike on the outside? We seem to like the same things on the inside, Rae Anne."

My sister didn't say anything. I scooted as close to her as I could get, but we were still in the front seat and there was a stick shift between us. I wanted to get her into the backseat. I wanted to make love to her so bad. Somehow she seemed more like my mother to me than my mother did. I could get close with Rae Anne, tell her things, whereas my mother put up that emotional distance unless she was drunk.

"It sounds like you must have had a really hard life," Rae Anne said, "not fitting in and being treated like you were crazy because you were different. I know Mom didn't want to give you up, but I think Grandpa did it because he thought it was going to be best for you, to give you a chance at a better life."

"How could being taken from my mother give me anything but a hole inside?"

Rae Anne stopped talking for quite a while. I didn't know what had happened. I couldn't figure out how to get the conversation back to pussies and fooling around without being obtrusively blunt.

Then she reached around in back of her and lifted out the bottle of gin. She opened it and drank a little of it straight.

"I want to talk to you about something," she said. "I've been trying to say it since that first day we met."

I leaned in close to her, my shirt hanging wide open, and I ran my hand lightly over her thigh. "What is it? You can talk to me. You can tell me anything, you're my sister."

"I had a baby last year, a girl. And I put her up for adoption. It was my choice. Mom begged me to keep her, but I thought I was doing what was best for the baby. I wanted to finish high school so bad, you know? I wanted to be more than just a dropout on welfare."

I wish I could tell you that Brenda Lee came over the radio at that moment, wailing sorrowfully about how *sorry* she was—it would have been so achingly poetic—but we were in Van Halen country. Anyway, the radio wasn't even on; the stars in the sky and the quiet night—murmuring of insects you can always count on but can never see were bittersweet enough in that dark car on that back road. We didn't need Brenda Lee.

I buttoned up my shirt and tried to control my sudden anger.

"I came so far," I scolded Rae Anne. "It took me so long to come home, and now it's like it doesn't even matter, because it's started all over again for that baby of yours."

I had pictures in my head of teaching Rae Anne a good lesson, of spanking her like a real mommy spanks her kid when the kid does something really wrong. A mistake, sure, but a mistake that hurts a lot of people and can never be undone.

"I fucked up," Rae Anne apologized. "I'm sorry."

swingers

Friday night I went home with some married people. I wish I could tell you they were those vibrantly tan, Hollywood fast-lane types, but they weren't. They were just married people. Intellectuals. Two married couples clearly pushing their mid fifties. I have to say, they weren't even very attractive. They certainly weren't fans of cosmetic surgery or fad diets.

You're probably wondering why I went home with them then. I'll tell you. They asked me to.

I was hanging out in one of those book bars. You know the one, the really well-lit place. Small and stuffy, with the built-in bookcases lining the walls, a teeny-weeny fire in the equally microscopic hearth. I was there being stood up. Nothing serious, though, no *tragédie d'amour*. It was just my intensely hyper garment industry–worker girlfriend who had stood me up. She'd obviously gotten snagged into working more overtime.

So I was alone in a surprisingly comfy chair, nursing a glass of red wine tentatively since I wasn't sure if I was just going to turn around and go home. That's when they walked in. Two unattractive married couples in their mid fifties. They made an instant commotion, boisterously dragging a tiny table around and scooting a bunch of comfy chairs together so they could all sit down and proceed to order an incredibly expensive bottle of wine. I loved watching that; the waiter trying to find somewhere to stand that was any-where near them while they ordered, and then having to set up an elaborate pedestal wine bucket somewhere in reach of them too. Thank God they smoked. They really needed some more stuff on that tiny table.

They couldn't help but notice me right away since they were practically sitting in my lap, and they kept trying to engage me in their small talk. I resisted their stabs at friendliness until they offered to share their wine, which necessitated their ordering another bottle. The waiter was really glad to see a fifth party, me, push into the already unmaneuverable fray.

So we got close in a hurry; we couldn't help it. Still, one of the women, Fran, seemed to impinge upon more of my personal space than I thought was really necessary. Right away I figured she was hitting on me. It took a couple glasses of that expensive wine before I realized they were all hitting on me.

I went home with them mostly because I couldn't believe they'd had the balls to ask me. They were so matter-of-fact about it too, like they always came on to younger, much more attractive single women, with great success. I was swept off my feet by their sheer blind optimism. Actually, I was swept off my feet by them, literally—I think they wanted to rush me into the nearest cab before I could change my mind.

We wound up in the home of the couple who lived closest to the bar. It was a really nice apartment. That couple, Cy and Ruthie, had never had any kids. Every extra penny had been avail-able for them to spend on themselves. They favored upholstery too. Everything was upholstered, in every conceivable pattern. I could tell an interior decorator had been paid handsomely to have his or her way with Cy and Ruthie. But I ceased noticing the decor when Fran started to undress me.

At first I felt alarmingly uncomfortable, because no one else was undressing. I shy away from being the only one naked in a crowd of strangers, so I was wondering what I'd gotten myself into. But after she'd stripped me naked, Fran pushed me gently down on the sofa and started massaging my feet. I began to relax. I sank deep into the upholstered sofa while Fran sat on the coffee table in front of me with both my feet in her considerable lap. Her hands were unexpectedly soft and steady. She worked each and every one of my toes and the balls of my feet with just the right amount of pressure.

She smiled encouragingly at me while the others just watched. I wondered if I was being lured into some exhibitionistic pas de deux with Fran. As I sunk deeper into the couch in an increasing state of bliss, I wondered how a group of people arrived at that sort of arrangement. "Hey, I know," I imagined them saying. "Let's all go out together, find a girl half our age, and watch her get frisky with Fran." There would be general agreement all around.

Then Fran broke my reverie. She lifted my foot to her mouth and sucked in my big toe. I was ready for it. Fran's mouth was so warm and wet I moaned. And slowly but surely, things started to move around me.

Cy got out of his chair. He came over and stood by Fran, his crotch level with her face. He unzipped his fly, but when he took out his dick it was flaccid. Completely limp. Fran didn't seem at all perturbed, but I felt a little indignant. I was thinking, *Hey, I'm naked here! The least you could do is worship me! Have a raging hard-on!* Alas, Cy was no longer nineteen, and Fran was apparently used to it. She went right to work with her mouth, alternating between my big toe and Cy's flaccid dick until remarkable things began to happen. It turned out Cy was hung.

Ruthie came over to join us then. She undid her husband's trousers completely, letting them fall rather dramatically to his ankles. Then, while Cy went to work on Fran's mouth with his stiff dick, getting her complete attention now as my feet lay limply in her lap, Ruthie kneeled behind Cy and seemed to be tonguing his ass. Her face was way in there, and I figured—as I watched his huge erection pumping in and out of Fran's mouth while his wife, fully dressed and on her knees, tongued his asshole—well, I figured that if I was Cy, I'd probably be liking that an awful lot. I got wet between my legs watching those three carry on like that.

Kenneth, Fran's husband, was the last to take the plunge, but suddenly he was sitting on the couch next to me and he was naked. He had a lot of hair. A touch more than I would have preferred. He didn't seem to notice that he didn't appeal to me, though. He lifted my arms and held my wrists together behind my head, then proceeded to lick my armpits. It was an unusual move, but it made my nipples shiver and get erect. Kenneth licked his way down to my breasts, and when his mouth closed around my erect nipple, I moaned again. Hairy or not, he was good with his mouth. My nipple swelled from the perfect pressure of Kenneth's sucking, and I decided at that moment that I ought to have sex with older people more often: They understood pressure.

The coffee table gang was starting to get rambunctious. Fran was flat on her back now as Cy straddled her on the low table, completely humping her face. She was making these eager but smothered little sounds that made it seem she was liking it a whole lot. And Ruthie had removed Fran's panties, pushed apart Fran's legs, and buried her face between Fran's fleshy thighs.

Kenneth's mouth was still working expertly on my nipples, moving from one to the other, tugging tugging tugging, but now one of his hands was also between my legs, rubbing my slippery clit.

I didn't think I'd be able to take much more of it; the free show on the coffee table and the perfect pressure on each of my three most responsive spots. I thought I was going to come.

That's when Cy startled all of us. He stopped humping Fran's face and went for her hole in a hurry. Ruthie had to get out of the way fast. She plopped down next to me on the sofa. She was the only one still dressed. She began to unbutton her blouse while Kenneth was rolling a rubber onto his erection. I felt a little overwhelmed. I didn't know who to focus on. It was obvious Ruthie wanted me to suck her fat little tits, but I was kind of hoping Kenneth was wanting his dick in me because I was definitely ready for it. That's when it occurred to me to quit sitting like a blob on the sofa and get a little assertive; get into the rhythm of being a swinger. Nothing was preventing me from having them both.

I turned over and raised my ass in Kenneth's direction while I let Ruthie guide my mouth to one of her jiggly tits. "Would you look at that tight tush," Kenneth declared as he slapped my ass hard. "Fran had a tush like that when I married her. Thirty years ago."

Then he mounted me. He slid his substantial hard-on into my soaking hole without any help from me. He slammed into my hole hard, making me cry out right away. He had a firm grip on my tush and was going to town.

Ruthie lifted my face from her breasts and started kissing me. Deep. Her tongue was crammed into my mouth while I grunted from the force of Kenneth's cock pounding into my pussy from behind.

I had never been with more than one person at a time before. It was kind of a scary feeling. I felt myself becoming insatiable. It wasn't long before I was flat on my back on the carpeting. Ruthie had stripped completely and was straddling my face. She had a tight grasp on each of my ankles as she kept my legs spread wide, giving Kenneth's hard cock free rein on my helpless hole, pound pound pound.

Ruthie's snatch was completely shaved. Her mound was smooth from the tip of her clit to the cleft in her ass. It had to be a wax job, I thought, she was that smooth. And I wondered: Who waxes a fiftyish woman's pussy completely bald? I figured her husband probably had something to do with it.

Cy was sitting in a chair now, sucking on a cigar, taking a breather, but his dick was still rock-hard. It was poking straight up like the Chrysler Building. Not that I could see him too well with Ruthie's ass in my face, but I knew that Cy was watching me get nailed. I was curious what he was thinking.

"I have to pee!" I suddenly announced as the urge came unmistakably over me. But my fellow swingers didn't miss a beat: They'd switched partners before I was even on my feet.

When I came back into the living room (and I hadn't been

gone long, mind you), Fran was down on all fours with Kenneth's hard-on seriously down her throat and Cy fucking her ass. The incessant pounding she was getting at both ends was making Fran's boobs bounce around like crazy. The whole thing was mesmerizing: what the men were doing to her and the way Fran seemed to be wildly into it.

❧

Ruthie came in from the kitchen with a tray of decaf espressos. She had that look on her face, like she'd had her orgasm and was feeling completely contented. She sat down next to me with her cup of espresso and we both watched Fran go the distance with Cy and Kenneth. And right when Fran started to jerk around and squeal, an indication that she was probably coming, Kenneth pulled his dick out of her mouth and shot his load in her face.

She seemed a little peeved by that, but she didn't do much about it because Cy was still going hog wild on her ass. I wondered if Kenneth was going to hear about it later, though, when he and Fran were home alone. I could hear Fran saying, "How could you come in my face like that?" I could tell she was capable of some serious chiding. "In front of everybody," she'd probably continue. "You know I hate it when you do that."

But for now everyone was amicable. Everyone was drinking decaf espresso except me. I hadn't come yet. I felt fidgety and distracted. Since I'd never been a swinger before, I didn't know the proper etiquette. Was it up to me to let everyone know I wasn't through yet, that I hadn't come?

I felt so ignorant, so ill-equipped to swing. I toyed with the idea of slipping off to the bathroom again, to take care of myself alone. No one would have to know what I was doing in there. I could come quick, I felt certain of that. Still, I felt, that was sure to be a letdown. I'd been having too much fun with everybody to suddenly resort to climaxing alone in some stranger's bathroom.

After only a few moments, it seemed as though coming alone

in Cy and Ruthie's bathroom wasn't even going to pan out. Fran and Kenneth were dressing. It was late, they said. They had a baby-sitter at home running up a fortune.

Then I wondered how old Fran really was if she had a child still young enough to need a sitter.

I figured I'd better get dressed too. I didn't want to overstay my welcome. I helped Ruthie clear up the remnants of the espressos while Fran and Kenneth left.

"I'll get your coat," Cy said to me. "I'll walk you down to the street."

"That's okay," I protested halfheartedly. My head was pounding. This swinging business had left my now-sober nerves a little raw.

"Nonsense. It's late. I'll walk you down."

Cy helped me into my coat and we got on the elevator. He pressed the button for the basement. I saw him do it. Maybe he was going to show me out the back way.

When the elevator doors opened, Cy led me down a narrow hallway and then out a door that led to the tenants' parking garage. It was dimly lit, with only a couple of naked bulbs burning.

"Look, you don't have to drive me," I insisted uncomfortably. "I don't live far. I'll get a cab."

"Why don't we get in my car anyway? I didn't come yet either."

I couldn't believe I'd heard him correctly. "What did you say?"

He looked at me and smiled engagingly. "I didn't come yet, either. I thought maybe I could persuade you to fuck around with me in my car."

I was stunned. I tried to feel affronted, but actually it kind of turned me on. The parking garage was deserted.

Cy unlocked his car door and we slipped into the backseat. "We'd better not undress all the way," he said, "just in case some-body sees us."

I agreed.

I climbed onto his lap and started kissing him. On the mouth. My tongue was shoving in deep. Cy's breath tasted like wine and espressos and cigars, and he suddenly seemed so grown-up. I felt incredibly attracted to him. "How old are you?" I challenged him. "Are you old enough to be my father?"

"Probably, why? Did you want to do a little role-playing?"

"Excuse me?" I didn't know what he was talking about.

"You know, I could pretend to be your irate father and slap your fanny really hard until we're both really hot. Then we could cross over that line together."

I didn't reply. I felt a little overwhelmed by how instantly appealing his idea sounded.

I let him maneuver me until I was across his lap. He methodically lifted my coat, lifted my dress and, with minimal effort but a nice, long lecture, he tugged down my tights, then my panties, and left them halfway down my thighs.

When my ass was completely bare and smack-dab over his knee, he let loose with a good old-fashioned spanking. The stinging, smarting kind.

"Shit!" I cried, trying to shield my ass.

But he wasn't at all deterred by my screams. He lectured me sternly on the perils of going home with perfect strangers, and behaving rather wantonly to boot.

I squirmed around in Cy's lap as I tried to dodge the steady, stinging slaps, but Cy kept them coming. He clamped my waist tight against his thigh and aimed directly for my helpless behind, which was heating up.

I could feel Cy's erection growing underneath me. He was really laying into me, spanking me hard, making me squeal out promises that I'd never misbehave again.

When my ass was completely on fire and I didn't think I could stand any more, Cy released me. He turned me over in his lap and unbuttoned the top of my dress. Slipping his hand inside, he worked my bra up over my tits and fondled my nipples. They were instantly erect.

I was still naked from my waist to my knees. The feeling of being so awkwardly exposed, my bare ass burning, while Cy fondled my breasts and tugged on my nipples made me want to get irredeemably dirty with him. But that was going to be difficult to do while keeping our clothes on.

I turned over and undid Cy's trousers. I unbuckled his belt and unzipped his fly, and his dick sprang out. I was happy to see it looking so lively. I buried my face in his lap, taking as much of his shaft down my throat as I could. I kneeled on the backseat with my naked ass in the air, not caring if anyone could see me. I was feeling unabashedly aroused. I sucked Cy's dick more fervently when I heard him begin to gasp and moan.

"Turn over," he said insistently. "Lie down on your belly." My bra was still up over my tits and the leather car seat was icy-cold against my nipples. It felt great.

Cy unrolled a rubber onto his erection and told me to raise my ass up a little.

I did.

My tights and panties still around my thighs, I felt his dick poking into my asshole. At first I thought he didn't realize he had the wrong hole, but he knew what he was doing. The lubricated condom slid into my ass without too much effort, but the pressure was intense.

"God," I groaned. Then I cried out uncontrollably while his huge tool went to work on my pitiful little hole.

"I hate to have to do this," he grunted, "you know that. But maybe this'll teach you not to go home with people you don't know."

"God," I was panting as he pounded into my stretching hole. "Jesus, God."

"Are you going to be a good girl now?" he continued, lifting my hips off the backseat and deftly sliding his hand down to my swollen clit.

"Yes," I whimpered while he rubbed my clit hard.

"Yes, what?"

"I'm going to be a good girl," I cried, as his cock seemed to swell in me even more, filling me to capacity with every thrust.

"And what happens if you're naughty again? What is Daddy going to do?"

"Spank me," I sputtered. "Daddy's going to spank me!"

"And what else?"

"Fuck my ass!"

"That's right," he concluded. "Daddy is going to fuck your ass." These last words he enunciated with amazing diction because he was coming at the sound of his own words. He slammed deep into my hole then and mashed me down on the seat. "Jesus!" he exclaimed with one last powerful thrust. "Jesus!"

And I was saying it too: "Jesus!" Partly because I was coming underneath him, shuddering and squirming against the leather seat; but mostly because I was testifying. I wanted my joy to be heard.

saturday night

On Saturday nights in the old days, I used to lie alone in my little bed in the dark and listen to the way my mother's stockinged thighs rubbed against each other as she walked shoeless down the carpeted hall. *Swish swish.* I heard her pass the open doorway of my darkened bedroom. The sound of silk against silk, more distinct than the sound of the TV droning faintly in the far-off living room, the noisy canned laughter barely reaching my ears. Those were the old days, the 1960s. The days when the money went farther. There was food in the refrigerator; it was joined by clinking bottles of beer on a Saturday night. It was home. It was safe. It was all that mattered.

Swish. Now I hear my own thighs rub against each other as I walk down my own carpeted hall. Because I can't afford silk, I wear nylon stockings. What I share with my mother from back then— who was younger then than I am now, still she seemed so mature, so grown-up—what I share doesn't stop with the stockings, the cold beer on a Saturday night. It's the rope we share, the hemp. Rough, scratchy knots that stay tied and get tighter when fought against. The struggle itself binds me to the bedpost tonight at the foot of the bed. My wrists are tied there, my knees up under me, my ass in the air. The stockings were removed hours ago. They lie now in filmy puddles on the bedroom floor.

It looks like the same ass, round and white. The same furrow of pubic hair peaking out, jet-black. It's just that it's me now and not my mother. It's *my* ass in the air. The sounds that I used to hear coming from her are now coming from me: groans of pleasure, animal grunts. An occasional whimper, a cry or two. The sounds that the ropes coax out of me came from another bedroom once, where a light spilled out from under a closed door, while I stood transfixed in the dark hallway and listened.

The burns that the hemp rope leaves around my wrists and ankles sometimes, I cover by wearing long-sleeved shirts and black stockings.

One July Fourth picnic, in my old backyard, stooping down to pick up a plastic fork I'd dropped in the grass, I glanced at my mother's perfectly manicured toes poking out of her low-heeled sandals. It was the first time I'd noticed the rope burns around her sturdy ankles. I looked up at her face in doubt; then her steady eyes met mine, as if she knew what I'd seen. I'd seen the burns before—not on her, but in photos of girls in strange magazines, a stack of which I'd discovered next to the hot-water heater in the basement. Picture after picture of white-trash women; women who weren't glamorous like the girls I'd seen in *Playboy*. These women wore little makeup. They were clad in only their white underpants and tied with rope. Some were struggling, some were smiling. Each magazine in the stack was a well-read issue of *Hogtied*. That July Fourth I went to bed wondering what it was going to be like to be a woman. It seemed scary. But I was excited when I thought of those girls in the magazines who'd been tied with rope. Was my mother like one of them? Was I going to be like her?

Now I put on sparkling earrings, I wear high heels. I drink martinis and wear smart black dresses. My lover shuns fancy cocktails. Like my father, he prefers to drink beer from a bottle. He follows me down the hall to our bedroom on Saturday nights, and he never tires of me. His strong arms wrap around me when he plants his parted lips on my mouth, shoving his tongue in. His kisses alone are enough to stir me, but his large hands usually slip under my dress and grab firm handfuls of my fleshy ass, shove my pelvis against his hard-on. He unzips my black dress easily, as if he could do it blindfolded, sliding it from my shoulders until it lies in a heap on the floor. My brassiere lands on top of the dress. Then he slips my feet out of my high heels and takes the rope from the closet.

We always end like this, with my wrists tied to the bedpost and my ass up in the air. But we start there on the carpeted floor, sometimes pretending he's an intruder who ties me to a chair, who then mauls my breasts eagerly while he makes me lick his balls. Sometimes we pretend he's just some guy, and I kneel in front of him and suck his cock. My hands are tied behind me then, and I rely on him to hold back my hair.

When we explore my white-trash roots, we really come alive. He'll tug off my garters and stockings and pull my panties down all the way. He'll toss me roughly across the bed, facedown, my long hair hanging over the side. He'll take advantage of my hands being tied and maneuver me under him. Then he'll call me a slut and fuck my ass and make me confess to being bad.

I own up to it all and grunt a lot. I strain at the ropes that tighten as I struggle, but I don't really suffer. I love this attention from my lover. Besides, it's in my blood to crave the rope: a Saturday-night tradition passed down to me from my mother.

the insomniac's tale

*Men have called me mad, but the question is not yet
settled whether madness is or is not the loftiest intelli-
gence, whether much that is glorious, whether all that
is profound, does not spring from disease of thought.*
—Edgar Allan Poe

    Curiously, as I lay here dying in the anonymity of
a Baltimore charity ward, trapped in the watchful
gaze of a stalwart nurse who seems, from time to
time, to regard me as if I'm already dead, I find I
have not a shred of remorse. In fact, if my vocal
chords—indeed, my entire larynx—weren't para-
lyzed by my rapidly deteriorating condition, I would
even go so far as to confess to my warden-nurse
what my true motivation had been. Why I'd fled the
train when it reached Baltimore, never proceeding
to Richmond where I was to wed Eloise Whitmore
within the next fortnight. I've ceased to feel shame
over any of it, yet I can't recollect when the shame
abandoned me. For the longest time, since the death
of my first wife seven years ago, it seemed the
shame was my sole companion. When did it leave?
Why is it gone so suddenly?
    I've no doubt now that somewhere during my
debauched excursion along the wharves of
Baltimore this very weekend I ingested a large quan-
tity of poison. Whether it was in the opium or the

cocaine; who gave it to me; and whether or not any of the prosti-
tutes I'd paid handsomely during the course of my debauch,
who'd perhaps watched me consume my fatal indulgence, knew
about the poison—well, these are the final mysteries I'll be taking with me to the grave.

Normally I'll pounce on a good mystery, unable to leave it be
until I've worried it like a bone, picked it clean and solved it. Now,
as the end arrives, I find I'm oddly ambivalent. These last mysteries are too meager, too petty to trifle over when compared with
the grander mystery that always fueled my life: my unconquerable
and insufferable destiny.

Every muscle in my face has now grown rigid with paralysis. I
can't so much as blink an eye. I'm terrorized by thoughts that I
will die with my eyes open. What horror will I see as one light
dims and perhaps the fires of Hell emerge? Whose face will be
my final vision as I pass over to the next realm? If God is merci-
ful, it will not be this dour face of my warden-nurse, a memento
only of this wretched charity ward. It will instead be the face of
an angel, my child-wife, a reminder of the beauty that could have
been life had I been born to a more regal fate. I fear I'll know the
extent of God's mercy soon enough: It is surely imminent, my
release from the fever of living.

I lay here unable to move as the paralysis creeps slowly through
me. How many hours has it been? When did they bring me here?
I no longer know. There's a certain timeless euphoria brought on by
abject misery. Meaning time passes strangely, an hour becoming an
unfathomable depth. In a way, life has always been a one-way tunnel. Still, it never seemed quite as linear as this certain encroach-
ment of death. Deeper into the tunnel I'm drawn, though, helpless
to fight death's pull. My mouth brimming with a bitter, corrosive
taste—not just from the hours spent vomiting up poison down by
the docks, but the bitterness of a final acceptance, a reluctant
understanding. A bleak awakening, if you will, to a truth too
unnerving to allow me ever again to know the blessing of sleep.

Had I been courageous enough to carry through on my vow to

marry Eloise Whitmore, had I proceeded on the train to Richmond, done the honorable thing, I wouldn't be in this hideous predicament. I know that. I'm always well aware of my failings. However, the drive to satiate my deeper urges pushed me from that train.

The youngest, freshest girls one can hope for often begin their lives of ill repute along those dank, rotting wharves of Baltimore. Some girls are so fresh they still carry the scent of home in their undergarments. To me their inexperience in the varied tastes of carnal lust matters little. I've long since tired of the meaningless couplings of body touching body. What I've come to seek is a peculiar sin, cultivated from the emptiness of too many years. A sin I can only reenact with the youngest of women, for I was with a young woman when my need first began.

My now-dead wife, once the love of my life, was a child of thirteen when I married her, though her mother had given us her full consent to wed. Then I was a man of twenty-four. Unlucky in my studies and my military career; unlucky in much of what had already passed as my life. Yet my literary prowess had begun to emerge. From the meager earnings I secured with my writing, I supported my child-wife and her mother, and we persevered. Hiding—successfully, I should add—a certain secret from the world.

In Boston, where I was born, I had been orphaned at the age of two. Years later in New York, no one I knew had ever known my mother, and thus no one knew that my mother-in-law had been my mother's sister. That she was indeed my aunt; and my child-wife, my cousin. But how I cherished the young girl I had taken for my bride. Not to marry would have been unthinkable. Never to join her, flesh pressed to flesh in the conjugal bed, seemed a fate unendurable to us both. Luckily, my aunt had a romantic and sympathetic heart of the most charitable nature, so she agreed to let us marry. In that, my bride and I were blessed. And in the facelessness of a bustling city such as New York, our sin—the incestuous nature of our marriage—was easily concealed. For a time, we even thrived.

In the beginning, yes, she was delicate, my wife. But she did not seem frail, though her skin was so sheer, so translucent that its pallor was decidedly tinted by the underlying blueness of her veins. Everywhere I touched her, she seemed impossibly soft—an unimaginable velvet—and too yielding to the merest caress.

It was hard to keep my thoughts fully centered on my work. I developed literary theories and wrote moody, atmospheric poems, which helped me to secure a certain fame, if not fortune, along the eastern coast. But always, the larger portion of my thoughts were devoted to (or perhaps I should say, tormented by) my enchanting wife.

Her modesty was such that throughout the course of our brief marriage, I never saw her by daylight entirely undressed. On occasion when we were alone, she might lift her skirt for me, or lower her blouse to bare her breasts. When under cover of darkness, if with luck a slash of moonlight would cut through the grimy windowpane at night and reveal her youthful wantonness sans nightclothes beside me in the bed, my eyes would desperately drink in the dim vision of her beauty. My other senses were driven to overcompensate for the sight of heaven of which my eyes were so deprived. The feel of her in my arms, her downy skin; her soft, tumbling tresses spilling across my chest; the flit of her feathery lashes against my cheek. Or the scent of her, her taste on my lips, the sounds of her awakening desire while we kissed—this was how my heart created its intimate portrait of her. How it aroused me; it was unspeakable. For there was yet another sweet agony I endured: My wife was still a child. Her womb had not yet reached womanhood. It lagged behind our eager needs. Thus our conjugal bliss was to be left unconsummated for two seemingly endless years. Until she reached the age of fifteen, when quite early on a stifling summer morning, the blood finally came.

It's hard to believe as I lay here, the paralysis approaching my lungs, my chest tightening, my heart a thin, miserable throb, that I could have once known such unbridled joy as the night my beloved wife and I endeavored to explore at last the full sanctity of our union. She was sweet, but not coy, determined to let me enter her as many times and in as many ways as I desired.

It seemed we were finally ready to face life, to stake our claim in the future. We had spent two years always moving, moving. I chased after employment with first one magazine then another, achieving more fame but still struggling to keep my little family from the jaws of poverty and hunger. But soon enough it became clear I would remain unlucky in this endeavor as well. My dear little girl, my wife, suddenly fell ill. Before long, we knew it was consumption, that lingering, wretched disease for which there is no cure. Malnourishment—a result of the poverty I alone had placed her in—aggravated her suffering. Seven times she slipped down to the worst depths of the disease. Only six times did she rally. With each of her slides down to the rim of death's abyss, I railed at the night and lost myself in drink, turning also to the comfort of opium or cocaine, behaving disgracefully around my peers, my public drunkenness severely damaging my hard-won reputation at banquets meant to honor me and my celebrated oeuvre.

Still, it was during these terrors, as I helplessly watched my poor wife wither, as I heard her cough and choke on her very blood, and knew without doubt that her release from suffering could come only with our final parting on this gruesome plane, that I wrote my finest tales of sheer horror—stories that sealed my fate in the pantheon of literature even while fortune continued to elude me.

My wife's mother and I were both at her side when she finally expired. My mother-in-law tenderly wiped the traces of blood from my wife's lips then attempted to remove the soiled dressing gown from her limp form.

"No," I insisted. "I want to be alone with her. You've nursed her all these years. Let me tend to her now."

When my mother-in-law left the room and I eased my wife's thin, lifeless body from the nearly threadbare chemise, my eyes weren't prepared to behold the heartbreaking beauty of her nakedness, a sight I had been deprived of throughout my marriage. How exquisite she was. Dear reader, I know you will be shocked by where my longings urged me! You, who have not known such bereaved misery as mine was—you could not be expected to comprehend the brutal power of love's erotic pull, even after death. I admit it plainly now. As I near death myself, I have no remorse. I hungered to know my wife's body in intercourse one final time. But could I dare it?

At first I thought no. I let my mind become submerged in the details of the task before me, attempting to let reason override the mounting pressure of my longing. I filled the wash basin and bathed the remnants of sweat from her once-fevered brow. Faithfully, I combed my wife's silken tresses. I sponged the length of her young body clean. Then I anointed her breasts with lavender and rose water.

My wife was just shy of sixteen the afternoon she died. The spectre of her purity, even in death, proved to be my undoing. Though I'd gone so far as to wrap my wife in her funeral shroud, when her mother knocked gently at the bedroom door I refused to let her reenter.

"I need to pray," I explained feebly. Then I turned the key in the lock, shutting out my last hope of sanity.

Had I known where it would lead me—the dark alleyways, the rotting wharves, the foul-smelling mattresses in vermin-infested rooms—had I known these curses would come closely on the heels of my indiscretion, would I have unwrapped my wife's still-supple body from the winding sheet? Would I have allowed my mouth to kiss hers as if she were still full of life and able to offer her lips to me? Would I have deliberately used that kiss as my invitation to cup the fullness of her breasts, then to enter her? And not just enter her, but part her legs garishly and watch my thick member violate her repeatedly as I pretended she willingly obliged me.

This is why the young whores of Baltimore are so well suited to my proclivity. I don't need experienced, licentious advances. I don't want vulgar women whose sexual openings are so well used as to seem lewd in how they gape. Though they needn't be virgins, I need fresh girls with a willingness to say "yes." To lay motionless and unstirred while I fondle and explore their secret places, first with my often trembling fingers, then with the more erotic caresses of my tongue.

Not that I had had nerve enough to know my wife's lifeless body in that intimate a manner. No, in the moments of my disgraceful assault on her, my mind was clouded with fever. I was fearful of being discovered at any moment by my wife's mother— my aunt, my own mother's sister; a witness to my debasement of her only child! Even while I knew the door was locked, in my mind it did not seem secure enough. An iron key in a simple hole did not seem an impenetrable barrier to the towering grotesqueness of the deed I was perpetrating. I kissed my wife's mouth, yes. And I squeezed her breasts, which were hardly warm. Yet when my erect manhood, seemingly of its own volition, proceeded on its mission to penetrate her, it was a deed I undertook in haste.

The sweeter subtleties of lovemaking, the gentler acts of fondling and caressing were not part of my assault. Not until the black midnight after my wife's burial, as I lay awake alone in bed, my thoughts tormented by the fresh memory of what I'd done to her, did my imagination give birth to its hideous cravings.

The sorrow of my loss was inexpressible. How I ached to have my wife alive again beside me. How I scourged myself for my financial impotence; my inability to lift her above the crush of poverty and the ravaging disease it delivered to her. It was in this swell of sadness that I began to regret not having lingered longer over her young body when it had still been a living, breathing vessel next to me; a body full of warmth and eager curiosity. As in the first days of our marriage, when every nuance of physical love was new to her and each intimate exploration a delight. Those early days when she was still too young for intercourse, when our nights were spent in ecstasy just the same.

Before my marriage I had known many women—mostly the

sort of women one pays. And I wasn't ashamed of this. In my years of approaching manhood I learned what I would be expected to teach my wife about lovemaking, and I learned the more carnal aspects of it that I would be expected to shield her from. It was my duty to her, and it was perhaps the only duty in which I served her well.

To ready a young woman's body for the demanding encounter of sexual penetration requires patience. But more, it requires dedication. I dedicated myself to my wife, to awakening her to her own capacity for sexual desire so that she would one day be ready for her final step into womanhood.

Yet how can I describe the veritable anguish of *my* desire? The nearly unbearable restraint I managed as I explored her youthful body in our bed, her nightclothes lifted for me, her legs eagerly raised and parted but her modesty prohibiting me from seeing her even in the glow of firelight. Her labial folds swelling under the touch of my fingers. My ears filling with the sounds of her passionate moans, her gentle cries, as my mouth between her spread legs urged her deeper and deeper into her own erotic abandon. Never to see her, to truly see her to my heart's content, in the usual female postures of lascivious invitation. Think of it! It must have been what drove me to do the unthinkable when my eyes were finally granted the full sight of her nakedness so soon after she expired.

Yes, it was ghoulish, the way the force of my thrusting member so disturbed and rattled her lifeless form. But my eyes shut it out. In the delirium of my sin, my eyes could only take in the beauty of her feminine secret; her vulva, at last exposed, revealed in the light of day.

After my wife was buried, the fevered thoughts that I'd assumed were satiated regrettably returned. I pictured it over and over in the dark: my thick and aching manhood glistening with my own spit as it pummeled into my wife's snug hole. My thoughts became diseased, replacing ideas of a more rational sexual fulfillment with notions of perverse lust. I berated myself for not having had the presence of mind to take more advantages with my wife's dead body while I'd been alone with it. Time and again I brought myself to ejaculation from the overwhelming erotic power of the vile urges that were in my head.

I became confused by the intimacy I'd experienced with my wife during our marriage and the foul deed I'd done to her after her death. I wanted to relive it all, but memory and fantasy became jumbled. I wanted my mouth again on her slick, swollen labia with her stiff clitoris, the tiny captive of my tongue. Or my fingers pushing deep into her secret holes. I even wanted the tighter posterior one, a thing I would never have asked from her in life. I wanted to "relive" things I'd never done with her! I wanted to experience that torrid liberation that I knew only briefly, the feeling that her body belonged solely to my lust, that I could do with it as I wished for she was dead and couldn't deny me.

Soon enough, the intensity of my passion increased. I started to seek the company of young whores in an effort to find release. "Just lay there, you understand?" I would say. "Don't move. Remain motionless while I undress you. Make as if you're dead. Then I want to do things to your body but you mustn't make a sound." At first, each woman would balk at my unexpected request.

I knew I must have sounded mad, as if I meant to jeopardize their bodily safety. I learned to pay the women their money in advance, while making it clear there was more money to be made if they could follow my instructions to the letter.

"You mean you expect me to lay here and let you have your way with me?" each young woman I propositioned would scoff, while always, without fail, eyeing the additional money.

"Yes," I would insist. "Don't move and don't make a sound."

In the ensuing silence of the girl's dank, putrid room, I would block out all things of the more rational world and allow my dark imagination free rein.

My literary pursuits, at long last, started to amass me a modest fortune. It was during a particularly bright period in my career that I met Eloise Whitmore. She was a decent, loving woman who was more my age, a woman who'd been tragically widowed in Richmond, and the younger sister of a writer I greatly admired. During a weekend visit to the writer's family estate, he introduced me to Eloise.

It wasn't long before a mutual spark of love ignited between Eloise and myself. For a time, her gentle dignity brought out the best in me. I proposed marriage. On the weekend that she accepted my hand, I fooled myself into believing I was a changed man. I was now engaged in more noble endeavors. I was through with my sickening preoccupations. No more time would I waste propositioning whores.

Though Eloise was an upstanding lady, the fact remained she was also a widow—a grown woman, well acquainted with the delights of the marriage bed. In what seemed at the time a harmless tryst—for it was understood we were soon to be married— Eloise and I decided to make love. I stole into her room late one night, where she was eagerly awaiting me in her bed. The rest of the household had long said good night. The entire house was in darkness.

In Eloise's room the lamp was still lit. She lay naked in among the sheets and the eiderdown. She had a robust, womanly figure that surprised and excited me. Full breasts, a voluptuous ass—so different from the young bodies to which I had become addicted. I slid into the bed beside her, kissing her ardently, entranced by her naked splendor.

She put a delicate finger to my lips to hush me. "Remember, we mustn't lose ourselves tonight," she whispered. "We have to be very careful. My brother's room is right next door. We don't want him to hear us." Then she proceeded to accept my unbridled sexual advances. Allowing me to know her in every position, including her mouth, but keeping silent the entire time.

It was her silence that unnerved me. It was her silence that baited me, even while I understood its necessity. It triggered the dark passion in me and provoked me to challenge her. I began to put her through her paces roughly, to see if I might elicit so much as a moan from her lips. She endured all my brutish passion with a compliance that bordered on subservience. Relentlessly, I drove the thick power of my manhood into her. She accepted its full force without a whimper. I even put her through the unthinkable: introducing my member to her anally. She struggled only briefly, then acquiesced.

It soon became apparent to me that even without the formality of the marriage vows Eloise regarded me already as her lord and master. It was a heady feeling, one I hadn't known since my first wife had died. It made Eloise Whitmore more enticing than ever. At the end of that weekend, I couldn't wait for Eloise to be my bride.

Why then, you must be asking, did it come to this, my imminent death by poison in a charity ward when I should be enjoying my most celebrated period of literary fame? And why my inability to resist the drink, the opiates, and the lurid pull of the young whores of Baltimore, when a woman of substance, of good breeding and a respected family, was waiting in Richmond to be my devoted wife?

The paralysis now squeezes hard about my lungs, shredding my final breaths. My warden-nurse has taken my right hand in hers, her fingers pressing firmly against the faint pulse in my wrist. As my eyes remain frozen garishly open, surely lending a mask of obscene horror to my face, I know now that God will have little mercy on me after all as I depart this miserable plane.

"It was to save her, you see!" I try vainly to scream at my nurse. But no sounds come. My thoughts are wedged tight against the thin ledge at the back of my barely sighted eyes.

It was to save Eloise Whitmore, who was so full of life, from ever discovering what I knew I would always hunger for.

Who comes now? A sudden face when all around has drifted into darkness. Listen to my tale, whoever you are. It was the body of a dead girl I cherished! It was the world between her legs! Not to marry would have been unthinkable, and so I took my cousin to be my child-bride.

anal

I knew a woman who had a virgin asshole until she was in her early thirties. I never understood that kind of woman; she's not at all like me. I'd read about *Last Tango in Paris* in my mother's *Cosmo* when I was only thirteen, for God's sake—and the accompanying article too, all about how to do it through the back door and, more important, why: Because a *Cosmo* girl is an American girl, and American girls love pressure.

I don't know if it was related to that article or not, but I dropped out of college in a real hurry, after only about six weeks. Something about wanting to feel alive instead, and that's how I ended up in New York; at the tail end of the disco era, pre-AIDS, a time when any self-respecting underpaid New York office worker drank heavily on his or her lunch hour and didn't have to be choosy about who he or she wanted to fuck when the work day was over—because eventually you fucked everybody. And there were so many exciting cross-purposes going on! For instance, drugs. Did you fuck somebody sheerly because s/he had the good drugs? Or did you use the good drugs as bait to get somebody to fuck you? Of course, if you hung in there long enough, the inevitable descent into hell finally occurred: You fell hopelessly in love with a completely insane person, but you were too fucked up on the good drugs to even notice it until a couple of years too late.

When it happened to me, it was with a woman. Back then, she was already twenty years older than me, so God knows if she's still alive now she's using a cane to get around. But she was in fine form in 1980—thin as a rail, of course, all bone, no muscle—but that was de rigueur in 1980. We didn't lift free weights. Every ounce of energy was reserved for lifting cocktail glasses off the wet bar (a long-distance endurance process) and for raising those teeny-weeny silver spoons, over and over…

So I'll call her Giselle. Her name wasn't anything close to that, but it *was* similarly unpronounceable and she possessed that quick, nervous energy sometimes, reminiscent of the leaping gazelle. And on our first date, when we hit on each other in that 10th Avenue after-hours meat rack and went home together to fuck like dogs, she was in fine, lithe, energetic form. I know we were kissing in the backseat of that cab, but I don't remember how we got from the cab to her sparsely furnished living room in that huge penthouse apartment in midtown, with the vaulted ceilings and all that glass. What happened from that point on is clear, though, because that's the sex part and all that matters anyway.

Giselle's husband was apparently loaded. And not one of those cash-poor types, either. He seemed to travel on business constantly—or so he said. At any rate, he was away an awful lot and Giselle had nothing but time and money to take his place. You'd think those two things—time and money—would have been enough, but when you're remarkably thin and nearly forty and beautiful and sharp and hopelessly underutilized like my dear Giselle, it takes a lot more than time and money to get your rocks completely off. Hence Giselle's insatiable drive toward the strange.

I'd agreed willingly from the outset. I had my clothes off in a hurry and was letting Giselle douche my ass, simply because she wanted it so much. I was happy to let her do it. I was on my knees and elbows in her half-bath, completely stripped with my ass in the air, a bulb syringe squeezing warm water into my rectum, a lit cigarette in one hand and a nice glass of merlot in the other.

When the water had done its trick and we were through making a mess in the half-bath, Giselle led me back to the living room and showed me the huge leather ottoman, how it lifted open for storing magazines and stuff. But she kept her bag of toys in there. It was a pretty big bag. That leather ottoman was sort of like a Playskool Busy Box for the seriously grown-up. When she'd emptied out the ottoman, Giselle encouraged me to bend over it so she could fasten my wrists securely to the wooden casters underneath. She even had specially made rubber wedges she'd shove under the casters to keep the ottoman from rolling all over the carpeting. Right away it occurred to me, when I saw the specially made rubber wedges, that it wasn't likely I was the first girl Giselle had stripped and douched and put over the leather ottoman. But I was okay with that. I drank like a fish and took a lot of drugs back then, so I was usually feeling pretty self-confident.

Once Giselle had secured my wrists, she inserted a steel thigh-spreader between my legs and buckled each padded end snugly around each of my thighs. And even though the thigh-spreader worked fine—it kept me from being able to close my legs—Giselle attached a padded ankle-spreader between my ankles too. I guess she just wanted to be extra sure. And then she came around the front of the ottoman to give me a hit off her cigarette and a couple of slugs of that great merlot.

My head was buzzing. I loved the feeling of being exposed—forcibly so. Giselle leaned over and kissed my mouth for a while, which made my naked backside squirm: When her tongue pushed around inside my mouth, it made me want to have her tongue poking into my hole.

"Look at this," she said.

She pulled a color Polaroid from a leather envelope and placed it on the floor under my face and went away.

I studied the Polaroid picture curiously. It was a picture of a girl much like myself. Well, it was impossible to tell if her face looked anything like mine, but she was totally naked and kneeling over the same ottoman, her legs forcibly spread in the same way, and she was tied down in the same provocatively helpless position. It could have easily been a Polaroid of me.

That's when I saw the familiar bright flash coming from behind me and heard the quick grinding sound of the inner workings of the camera. In a mere sixty seconds, the color Polaroid in front of me was replaced by a color Polaroid of myself. The similarities were uncanny.

We didn't talk any more after that. Giselle gave me a couple of quick swigs from my glass of merlot and one last drag off the cigarette, then she slipped the gag into my mouth. Tied it pretty tightly, I must say. One of those knots where you just know your hair's a big gnarly mess in back.

Giselle got undressed somewhere, out of my field of vision. I couldn't see her. But when she straddled my back, her slippery pussy was sliding all over my skin. It was obvious she was naked. She leaned down and spoke in my ear confidentially, as she replaced the picture in front of me with one of yet another girl.

"She's awfully pretty, honey, don't you think? Her asshole's so tight, would you look at that? Incredible, isn't it?"

I grunted and nodded my gnarly head in agreement.

"Not even a hint of a hemorrhoid, see? This girl's in great shape."

I have to admit, I was a little transfixed; such vivid close-ups! Giselle had obviously invested a fortune in her camera lens.

"She was very well-behaved, if I remember correctly," Giselle went on. "She took it like a champ, that one did. You think you're going to be a good girl too? Huh? You've been awfully accommodating so far." Giselle began to kiss my neck slowly and she rubbed her wet pussy all over my lower back. "What do you think?" she repeated. "You think you're going to be a good girl?"

"Uh-huh," I grunted through my gag. I was going to be a very good girl. I was going to be stellar.

anal

"You like things in your ass? You've had things in your ass before, right?"

I nodded my head yes, but I confess I felt a little tripped up; what did she mean by "things"?

Then a different Polaroid was put in front of my face, a slightly more startling one. "Same girl," Giselle whispered, "but do you notice anything different about her?"

It's a huge gaping hole, I thought nervously.

"This is how her asshole looked when I was through appreciating her. Pretty remarkable, isn't it?"

Giselle brushed some stray hairs affectionately from my forehead, I guess to make sure my vision wasn't obscured in any way. I was riveted to that Polaroid, the crystal-clear close-up of that well-used sphincter.

"Of course, this sort of appreciation takes a few hours," Giselle explained. "You don't have to be anywhere for a while, do you?"

I don't think I really responded to that, I was a little too mesmerized by the photo. She left it on the floor in front of my face and then disappeared somewhere behind me.

The anticipation is always the greatest part, isn't it? Man, you're just waiting and waiting and you don't even know what the hell *for.* But you feel real certain that you're going to get it, that it's eventually going to come. And that's the sort of excitement I was feeling; like some mad ferret had chewed his paw free from a steel leghold trap inside me and now he tore wildly around in the darkness of my intestines, wanting very much to find his way out. But that was 1980. You *know* I was young. I was still excited by things like suspense and fear, and the chance to get my asshole reamed by a seriously grown-up girl.

It started with a simple strawberry. A bright red one with a long stem. Giselle had straddled my back again and lowered the long stem down in front of my face. She twirled it gently, holding the stem between her thumb and forefinger. "What do you think?" she asked. "Can you take it? It's not too big, but it's awfully fragile."

161

In an instant the bright red berry was gone and Giselle slid her slippery pussy slowly down my back, until I imagined she must have been on her knees between my spread thighs. The tip of the berry was icy cold when she pressed it against my tight hole, and I could feel my asshole clench even tighter. It was an involuntary reaction to the icy intrusion.

"I can see I have my work cut out for me," Giselle announced solemnly. "We could be at this a *long* time."

I felt something sticky dribble down the crease in my ass. It oozed slowly, like honey. And I think that's just was it was. When the slowly dribbling drop inched toward my clenching asshole, Giselle's tongue was there to meet it. She pushed the sticky substance around and around, all over my anus. The stickiness felt strange; it was lightly pulling at my hole. But the warmth of her tongue, pushing into the tight opening now and then, felt good. My hole definitely liked that. When Giselle had licked the surface of my asshole clean, she dripped another trail of honey down the crack of my ass. Again, it oozed so slowly down that I felt this alone, this waiting on the honey business, could in itself take hours. My ass wriggled and squirmed impatiently, perhaps trying to assist the honey in its journey down, but when the honey finally reached its destination, and when Giselle's warm tongue was once again there to greet it, the honey felt even more appealing than it had the first time. I felt my sphincter muscle eagerly anticipate her poking tongue. I moaned into my gag and arched my ass open for her.

"This is definitely progress," Giselle announced quietly. "But let's not rush it. You're not really ready for the berry yet."

Giselle came around in front of me and I watched her polish off my glass of wine. She sat, naked, and lit a cigarette.

"I know how to remedy this, though, so don't lose heart," she said. "It takes patience and then you'll be able to get anything you want in there. Even something like a strawberry."

I watched her as she thoughtfully smoked, and even though I didn't have some long list of things I'd been trying to get *in there,*

I suddenly felt like I desperately wanted to please Giselle. I wanted anything in my ass that she wanted to put in there. My hips were rotating restlessly against the ottoman while I watched her smoke. I could feel the wetness in my vagina beginning to drool down into a puddle on the carpeting. I didn't know what she had in mind for me, but I had a pretty good inkling that my ass was going to get fucked good by this gorgeous, skinny woman who, let's face it, was technically old enough to be my mother.

When she finally stubbed out her cigarette, I watched her snap on a latex glove. I'd never seen anybody wear gloves like that before, except the doctor in the examining room, and watching her snap it on made my stomach a little queasy. I wanted to ask her where she got gloves like that, but I had that gag stuck in my mouth and couldn't say a word. But when she disappeared again behind me and, without much fuss, slid a lubed finger up my ass, I wasn't thinking about buying gloves. I just gasped. Well, I moaned a little bit too. She worked that latexed finger into me deep. And it was so slick with lube, my tiny hole couldn't put up any kind of resistance. It tried to push against the intrusion, but Giselle was insistent. She worked against the pushing hole. She slid two fingers in, in fact, and pumped them vigorously in and out while I grunted a little and tried to figure out whether or not I liked it.

But I didn't have a lot of options; I was spread open for her either way. She paused for a moment and squirted the lube directly into my hole. It was an icy and unpleasant feeling, but the sensation didn't last long. It was replaced by the less subtle intrusion of three greasy fingers this time. Giselle was exerting herself, I could tell; she was grunting from the effort of pumping her three fingers against the muscle that was trying to expel her.

"Jesus," I gasped into my gag. And my eyes were riveted to the picture on the floor in front of me. That gaping hole. It was going to be mine before morning came and I was sickly curious about how we were going to achieve this.

"Are you ready to pick up the pace?" she panted. "Are you ready for some action?"

Of course I couldn't answer her, and I guess she didn't really
expect me to, but Giselle came around in front of me then and let
me watch her strap on the dildo.

"What do you think?" she asked urgently. "Can you handle this
guy?"

She was referring to the dildo, to its overall size. But I was too
caught up in looking at her. I'd been with girls before, and girls
with dildos too, but I'd never been with a woman yet who had
actually strapped one on. Giselle looked hot. I was eager again.

"What do you think?" she persisted, as if she'd forgotten about
the gag. "You think you can take him?"

I grunted my urgent approval as I watched her lube it up. "Uh-
huh," I grunted several times, and I even nodded my head.

And when she climbed onto me, mounted me, pressing the
lubed head against my asshole, easing the dildo into my rectum,
it was like I was fourteen again and I was with that boy. We'd
skipped school and we were hiding in his father's den. It was dark
and very quiet in there. Their maid was home, but she didn't
know we'd skipped school and snuck back into the house. We had
decided we were going to do this thing, we were going to try it
out. We were determined. And I'd brought my torn-out article
from my mother's old *Cosmo* and my plastic jar of Vaseline in my
shoulder bag. We didn't get undressed because we were afraid of
needing to leave in a hurry. So we just unzipped his fly and took
his hard dick out. We smeared Vaseline all over that thing. And
then I leaned into one of his father's big leather club chairs, my
face pressed against the cool leather, while the boy shoved up my
skirt and pulled my panties down to my knees. Vaseline makes
everything a greasy mess, especially nice leather club chairs, but
it sure helped that boy's hard-on slide right into me, right into my
asshole. It was like we'd talked about over the phone; he was
actually fucking my ass. I wasn't sure I really liked it, but I wasn't
sure I didn't like it either. The pressure felt exciting, I liked the
feeling of being filled up. But what I liked most was his fully
clothed weight on top of me while my panties were around my

knees, and the way he smelled while he grunted and pumped away at my virgin asshole, the way all boys smelled back then: like mown grass and sweat and tobacco and spearmint gum.

That was how it felt with Giselle, like I wasn't really sure I liked it, but I wasn't sure I didn't like it either. The dildo felt huge in my ass and I was grunting into my gag. But her naked weight was on top of me. Her breasts were pressed flat against my back and she was sweating from the effort of pounding me. I loved all that sweat. And I didn't mind it when she pulled the dildo out and reminded me I wasn't fourteen anymore and that it was 1980: She shoved a glob of Crisco up my ass and proceeded to pump me with a dildo too huge, too heavy to even attempt to fit into the harness. Giselle didn't strap it on, she held it with two hands and shoved it clear down to its base, stretching me completely open.

I groaned like some drugged animal giving birth in a public zoo, but I was loving every minute of it. The Crisco made it easy on my hole. I opened right up and accepted every round rubbery inch of the fake dick that Giselle pounded so mercilessly into me.

And my eyes were still glued to the photo in front of me. I was suddenly in love with the mystery girl in the Polaroid. I knew now what had stretched her open, I knew now how she must have felt—spread wide and securely battened down. A gag probably shoved into her mouth too so she could grunt over and over in it as her rectum was filled to capacity, her ears filled with the sounds of Giselle's own grunting from all her strenuous effort.

When Giselle had worn herself out she disappeared briefly into the half-bath then reemerged with a soaking towel. The towel was hot and felt great against my tired hole. And when Giselle had wiped away most of the grease, there was the familiar bright flash again behind me and the sound of the grinding inner workings of the camera. By the time she'd untied my gag, the new photo was ready.

"What do you think?" she asked softly, as she laid the Polaroid of my seriously opened hole on the floor in front of me. "You think you can handle that berry now?"

I'd forgotten about the strawberry. "I suppose so," I panted, although I wasn't entirely sure.

"I'll wedge it in with a little honey and then I'll eat it out of you. But I want to get a picture of it first. My husband loves these pictures," Giselle explained, "the ones with the food in the girls' asses. He carries them in his overnight case and takes them all over the world."

I wasn't sure I was particularly pleased with that idea, but I couldn't keep Giselle from wedging that sticky strawberry in me. It took it easily this time, the berry perched right there in my puckered anus. Then the camera flashed away. I wondered what her husband looked like; would I ever see him on the street? Would it haunt me that somewhere in the world a man was flying from place to place with a picture in his overnight bag of me with a strawberry in my ass? And what about the mystery girl in the other Polaroid? What kind of food had ended up in her stretched hole?

But my worries melted away when Giselle's mouth found the berry. True to her word, she nibbled it out. She plucked the stem clean and then sucked the berry and gnawed it and licked it until it was gone.

"Come on," she said, as she undid all the buckles and restraints, "let's go to bed. Let's make a little love."

She refilled my wineglass, but I didn't want it anymore. I just wanted to be flat on my back underneath her on her big bed. The sun was just coming up in all those enormous penthouse windows, so when she straddled my face for some sixty-nine I could see her asshole clearly. It was stretched like mine, but hers was permanent. She lowered it right onto my tongue while she shoved my thighs apart wide and buried her face between my legs. Her hot tongue licked at my tender, aching, worn-out hole, while her fingertips deftly massaged my clit. I tried to rub her clitoris too, but she didn't seem to want that. She seemed content to just ride my tongue with her open hole.

I licked her asshole with all the earnest attention I could give her, but after a while, I must confess, the way her mouth was making me feel between my legs absorbed more and more of my concentration. I couldn't give Giselle the amount of attention I should have. While her fingertips slipped all over my swollen clit, and while her tongue licked eagerly at my played-out asshole, I couldn't help myself, I came. I dug my fingers into Giselle's gorgeous ass and clamped my thighs tight around her head and came.

And since it was 1980, I didn't stay the night with her. I stumbled into my clothes and left. I kissed her goodbye and all, but then I went out alone for breakfast.

A couple nights later she called me. "My husband's in Thailand," she said. "What do you say we go at it again? Are you up for it? You're not still sore, are you?"

My asshole quivered. "No, I'm not sore," I said into the receiver.

"I have some new things that we could try putting up there. Are you game?"

And I realized I was. It was the beginning of my inevitable descent into hell with a completely insane person. "I'm game," I confessed.

"Good," she said quietly. "Be a doll and pick up some film. Now how do you feel about root vegetables?"

judge johnson's will

Camellia Johnson, age sixty-five, did what she always did first thing every morning: She tugged gently on the expensive silk window shade and raised it to reveal the rising sun. On this morning, however, she was up a little earlier than usual. On this morning she was different. For this was the morning after the apocalypse. The morning that had lain dormant within every other morning she'd faced in her adult life; like clockwork, it had come. Her husband had died during the night, and now Camellia Johnson was a widow. The dread of this day had been racing toward her at the speed of light since the very moment she'd nervously uttered her marriage vows at 5:55 P.M. on Saturday the fourteenth of June, 1952, at First Methodist Church on Main. She'd been auspiciously declared the wife of Judge Percival Whitehead Johnson, a man in questionable health who was nearly twenty years older than she was. The dread filled her now as she faced the morning alone, but the dread too was somehow different.

Empty, Camellia realized. Being a widow felt nowhere near as tragic as she'd always anticipated.

She opened the door to her husband's adjoining bedroom and entered solemnly, taking in every nuance of the now-silent room, letting it envelop her doubting senses before she let her eyes light, once again, on the lifeless body of Percival.

There he is, she thought. *Well, his body, anyway.*

At 4:10 that morning, Judge Johnson had been pronounced dead of heart failure and Camellia had become, officially, the richest person in Hernville; male or female, young or old.

He doesn't look like he's sleeping, like they always try to tell you, Camellia thought to herself as she studied his lifeless form, his lower body tucked neatly under the deep ruby heirloom eiderdown. *Peaceful or not, he looks just plain dead.*

She picked up the phone and dialed 411, too lethargic and sleep-deprived to reach for the phone book on the shelf of her husband's night table and find Skoff's number herself.

"What number, please?"

"Skoff's Funeral Parlor," Camellia replied.

She was given the number she needed, but not before Hilda Kurtz, the operator on the other end of the line, added disingenuously, "So very sorry to hear about the judge, Mrs. Johnson. You have my deepest sympathy."

I wish I had all your money was what she was trying to say, and Camellia knew it.

"I appreciate that," Camellia replied just as falsely. Thinking, as always, how repugnant it was that the minute-by-minute occurrences in her complicated life could keep the small wheels of petty envy ever-whirring in the minds of useless people like Hilda Kurtz, even at 7 in the morning, before the death knell had even tolled. The ignorance behind such petty envy disgusted Camellia. "Spare me your sympathetic horseshit," she wanted to spit at Hilda, who'd been relentlessly envious of Camellia since they'd graduated in the same class together nearly fifty years ago. "Do it already, you stupid bitch. Go find out for yourself; find some rich sitting duck and fuck him into marrying you, if you're so sure that's what's given me a better life than yours for the last forty-seven years, you piece of shit."

Instead, Camellia said nothing more. She was a woman who had learned that the larger part of grace, especially if one was married to the richest man in Hernville, was in keeping one's misery to oneself. She clicked the receiver for a new dial tone, then rang Skoff's Funeral Parlor.

John Skoff Jr. would be awake already, she knew. He would have been called earlier by Dr. Elliot, forewarned that the Honorable Judge Johnson was dead and would be needing a spot in the refrigerator.

"Or whatever they call it," Camellia said under her breath.

"Good morning—Skoff's."

"John, it's Camellia."

"Yes, Camellia, I thought it would be you. How are you managing?"

"Fine."

"I thought I'd send a vehicle around in an hour, about 8. Is that okay for you? Will you be ready by then?"

"Yes, John, that's fine. I'm ready."

At sixty-eight years of age, John Skoff Jr. was three years older than Camellia. Over fifty years had passed since John and Camellia had gone out on their only date. It had been Camellia's first unchaperoned evening with a boy. She'd been fifteen. It was well after the Second World War, about a year after her older sister, Pearl Anne, had been killed in a hiking accident. Even though Camellia had felt perplexed, unable to fathom why an older boy like John Skoff would want to take Camellia out on a date, the evening had gone well until John had suggested they sit in his car for a while and kiss.

John was Camellia's first hard lesson learned about dating: No matter how exciting it feels, don't let a boy fondle you under your clothes if you want him to date you again.

Camellia had been hurt when John Skoff Jr. never telephoned for a second date. In her ignorance of how to play the game of sex, Camellia had been audacious enough to enjoy what she and John had done together in his car and had eagerly anticipated another evening of bliss with him. In fact, she'd practically fallen in love. When John Skoff never called again, Camellia had found another reason to mourn Pearl Anne's passing. Camellia missed the easy confidences she'd shared with her older sister. In the past, she'd relied on Pearl Anne for advice. When Camellia had naively confided in her mother that more than a good-night kiss had passed between her and John, a black cloud of anger had passed over her mother's face.

"You should be ashamed of yourself, acting like a whore," Camellia's mother had scolded after closing the bedroom door in order to spare Camellia's father the awful news. "No wonder the boy doesn't want to see you again! He comes from a decent family. He probably mistook you for a girl who had been raised in a good Christian home!"

Until the demeaning exchange with her mother, it hadn't occurred to Camellia to feel ashamed about what she'd done with John Skoff. And even though she did dutifully begin to feel ashamed, she wasn't sure why. The word "whore" confused her. She'd rarely heard it used and had never fully understood its meaning.

Early the following morning, while the household slept, the fifteen-year-old Camellia snuck into her father's study and consulted his massive dictionary. "Whore," it read, "noun: A prostitute. A sexually immoral woman." Camellia was no more enlightened than before. She'd returned to her bedroom feeling dirty just the same and forever after would feel a mild sense of uneasiness at the mere sight of John Skoff. And now the uneasiness had returned at the sound of his voice on the phone.

Let it go, Camellia, she thought to herself. *It was too many years ago. Nobody even remembers it now.* She said goodbye to John Skoff Jr. and hung up the phone.

The phone was no sooner back on its hook when it rang. Camellia glared at it. An intrusion, she thought, feeling alarmed. Probably the *Hernville Reporter*. No, it was too early for the press, she realized. The phone rang again.

She answered tentatively. "Hello?"

"Camellia, it's Hank. I just heard. Should I come over?"

Camellia was relieved. "Yes, Hank, come over. I'm waiting on

Skoff's drivers now. I think I'll put on some coffee. Have you had coffee yet?"

"A cup of coffee would be great. I just this second woke up. Hilda Kurtz called, of all people, and told me about Percy. I'll throw on some clothes and be right over."

Hank McGwynne had been Judge Johnson's trusted lawyer for the last thirty years. He handled every aspect of the judge's vast estate. Not only Percy's hefty earnings as the town's only judge but the formidable holdings of Percy's inherited family fortune as well—Hank oversaw it all. Additionally, he was the only person in the whole town of Hernville to whom Camellia could turn as a friend, in whom she could always confide. It was Hank who had recently saved Camellia from an awkward fate, a scandal that would have been hotter than any scandal the pathetic town of Hernville had yet seen.

It had happened only two weeks ago.

Hank McGwynne had paced the floor of his spacious office. He had bitten his lower lip, furrowed his brow, and paced some more. When he stopped pacing, he'd sat agitatedly at his desk and rapped his expensive pen sharply against the hard mahogany.

How could he do it, he wondered. How could he betray the confidence of Percival Whitehead Johnson, his most prestigious client? *Fuck the client aspect,* he argued with himself. *He trusts me as a friend.*

Hank couldn't let it go, though. He couldn't stand by and watch Camellia be humiliated. But he would have to approach her in secret—contrive to run into her by accident and then convince her to meet him alone somewhere. He couldn't even risk a casual phone call to Camellia at home; anything out of the ordinary might alert Percy that a betrayal was under way. The old coot was nearly eighty-three, but he still had a keen and suspicious mind.

Hank had studied his daily planner and then hit on an idea. He would have his secretary, Miss Carver, call the downtown salon where he knew Camellia had her hair washed and set every week. When Miss Carver had procured the day and time of Camellia's next appointment, Hank endeavored to cross paths with her.

"I need to speak to you alone," he told Camellia under his breath on the day of the contrived meeting. "Privately," he stressed. "It's important."

When they were safely sequestered that evening in a hotel suite two towns over, Hank put it to her plain: "Percy has another young one."

Camellia shot him an irritated glare. "Is that *it*? 'Another young one'? Is that what this is about, Hank? Why the cloak-and-dagger secrecy?" she demanded. "And all the driving, for God's sake. You could have told me a thing like this downtown."

"This time it's different, Camellia. Percy had me change his will. *This* whore will get a significant portion of his fortune if he dies today."

Camellia was stunned. "Who is 'this whore'?"

"Lydia Lee."

Camellia stared at Hank in disbelief, a wave of nausea washing over her. "Lydia Lee? Why on earth would Percy be willing to consort with a piece of blond trash like Lydia Lee?"

"Camellia, I can honestly say I have no idea. I assume it's the usual."

"When did he ask you to change his will?"

"Two days ago. And he insisted on waiting while I revised it. He wanted it signed on the spot, in case he keeled over on the golf course, I guess."

However, Camellia thought now, as she sat down next to her lifeless husband's shell of a body on the large, imposing bed, he hadn't keeled over playing golf. His heart had given out while she, Camellia, his wife, had been between his old, knobby legs. Her breasts spilling out of a bright crimson satin teddy that had felt two sizes too small, his half-limp manhood in her lipsticked mouth. But by then, the will had been changed back at Percy's request, signed and witnessed, and Camellia had been reinstated as Percy's sole heir. It had been a degrading two weeks for Mrs. Camellia Johnson, but financially it had paid off in spades.

&

At the other end of town, Deputy Sheriff Dil Glenn took his cup of coffee into the dark bedroom and poked Lydia with his finger. He poked her again when she didn't stir and then he lightly shook her. "Lydia, wake up. I just heard some news on the radio."

Lydia's puffy eyes opened and she strained to focus on what Dil was saying.

"It sounds like the old geezer kicked."

"What?" Lydia replied.

"Judge Johnson. He's dead."

"You're not kidding me, are you, Dil? You wouldn't joke about something like that?"

"No, baby," he grinned. "I just heard it on the radio."

"He's really dead? The old fucker's dead?"

"Yeah, Lydia. You're going to be richer than shit."

"Hell, yes," Lydia agreed, reaching out for Dil's arm. "Richer than shit. Put down that coffee and fuck me, hon. I suddenly feel like celebrating."

&

Camellia splashed her face with cold water and then studied herself in the bathroom mirror. She was startled to see her lips still faintly stained with the cherry-red lipstick Percy had insisted she wear. The same cherry-red lipstick that had been smeared on Percy's shriveled member when Dr. Elliot had come upstairs, examined Percy's body, and pronounced him dead. Camellia had been too distraught to think straight and hadn't even noticed the lipstick smears on Percy's private parts until it was too late.

How humiliating, she realized now. But she would find a way to cope with it because now she was the richest woman in Hernville.

Downstairs the doorbell chimed. It was too early for Skoff's drivers. It was probably Hank.

174

≈

John Skoff Jr. watched his drivers ready the back of the ambulette with a gurney and a fresh black bag. He was glad it wasn't Camellia. That he wasn't ready to deal with. In fact, he hoped he himself would be dead and buried before it was time for the hearse to carry her.

When the ambulette was out of sight, John walked upstairs from the mortuary to his living quarters. In the kitchen, he pulled open the refrigerator door and examined its contents, deciding on eggs for breakfast.

His partial erection nudged his trousers.

No, he told himself. *This can't be happening. It's not happening, I'm too old.*

But his erection persisted, until it had swelled to proportions he couldn't ignore.

≈

Dil had a firm grip on Lydia's wide, fleshy ass as he watched his thick cock pound into her. He loved to listen to her animal sounds, her carnal cries of lust. He purposely went at her harder, knowing she would arch her fat ass even higher when he did so, making for a gorgeous view.

Lydia's tousled blond hair hung down in her face wantonly as her backside took the force of Dil's pounding. "Shit, Dil," she gasped, holding tight to the pile of pillows beneath her, her teeth sinking into one of them as she grunted in sync with Dil's piston-like rhythm.

Lydia lost herself in her lust, thinking of Cal now, of how she would show him once and for all. He was always mocking her, laughing at her, deriding her for her silly get-rich-quick ideas. Well, she'd show his black ass now; he wouldn't be laughing for long when he learned that she was loaded.

"Let's do Cal," she grunted out suddenly.

"What?" Dil asked.

Lydia craned her neck to look back at him. "I said, let's do Cal. Let's do another three-way with Cal."

"You know I don't like you fucking those black boys, Lydia. Besides, he's in jail."

"Well, get him out, it's only a vagrancy charge."

"I can't get him out, girl. I'm just a deputy."

Lydia uncoupled from Dil abruptly, turned over, and gave the predicament some thought. "Well, then let's do it down at the jail. Better yet, why don't you fuck me in front of the bars of his cell and really make him suffer."

Dil eyed her uneasily. "You're not serious?"

"Shit, yes, I'm serious; why not? We can do it when Sheriff Palmer's at lunch or something. And if Cal decides to flap his gums about it, who's the sheriff going to believe: You or Cal?"

"I don't know, Lydia. Seems to me, you're asking for more trouble."

"Not anymore I'm not, because I'm going to buy me the biggest house in town and put up a fancy iron gate and then hire an armed bodyguard, twenty-four hours a day. And Cal's nasty black ass won't be able to get near me unless he has an invitation."

"And what about me?" Dil asked as he zipped his now-limp dick back in the trousers of his uniform and prepared to go to work. "Where am I going to be living during all this?"

"With me. We're getting married, Dil, right?"

"I suppose so, if you can quit stewing about Calvin long enough to say 'I do.'"

❧

John Skoff Jr. walked down the hallway of his house to a room he rarely stepped foot in anymore, the bedroom he'd had as a boy. He stood in the doorway and studied its emptiness. The early-morning sun shone in on the faded carpeting. Everything from his childhood was gone. The furniture he'd given to his nephew, his sister's boy, after both their parents had died and John had moved into the front bedroom. John had discarded every last memento, every scrap of history that had been connected to his boyhood. He had either given it to charity or tossed it in the trash years ago. As he studied the empty room now and felt his erection insistently push against his trousers, he knew that his adolescence still lingered. Even though half a century had passed and the room was as good as dead, he couldn't annihilate the essence of the boy he'd been.

John walked back up the hall to the front bedroom. He went in and sat down on the bed that had once belonged to his parents. The bed he was probably conceived in. For some reason he had kept all their mementos while dismissing his own. John looked around the room at all the things that had been his father's. His mind went past the bedroom walls and considered the other rooms, the rest of the house, and the mortuary itself. It had all been his father's once; even John's name had first belonged to his father. But all these trappings didn't make him his father, he realized, even though he had made a gallant effort to become him.

John stretched out on the bed and thought of Camellia. It wasn't long, though, before his thoughts skipped over Camellia and settled on her long-dead sister, Pearl Anne. And then the damage was done. John lowered his fly and retrieved his erection, surprised and sickened at how responsive it was, even after all these years.

Pearl Anne. He'd loved Pearl Anne from afar all during high school. Her light chestnut hair had hung in waves down her narrow back, seeming always to point to her cute derriere and filling his loins with longing. He'd never had courage enough to say much more than hello to Pearl Anne, and so his amorous intentions had gone unrequited.

The summer John turned seventeen was when Pearl Anne had been killed in that fall she took while hiking out at Lake Hernville. John had been devastated by the loss like the rest of the town, but perhaps even more so since he had worshiped her so keenly. And though he should have expected it, it was instead a gruesome shock when he heard the hospital ambulance pull up to the mortuary's back door and saw the drivers bring in the lifeless body of Pearl. It was hard enough to keep his mind off that, as he stayed hidden in his room upstairs, but when he heard Pearl Anne's mother arrive later that day bringing the clothes Pearl Anne would wear to the grave, it became too much for John's mind to handle. He plunged into a morbid torpor in which he fixated on the thought of the dead body of the girl he loved only one floor below him.

That evening, he didn't join his family at the dinner table. He wouldn't have been able to converse with them. He felt incapable of leaving his room, plagued by a mild, unceasing nausea. He lay on his bed and mourned for her. She was all alone in a dark drawer, cold and helpless and—

"And what?" he'd wondered aloud. He knew his father had yet to begin his work on her. She wouldn't be wearing her burial clothes yet—what was Pearl Anne wearing inside that drawer? Was she naked? His mind skittered clear of the disquieting thought, but the dark pull of it proved to be magnetic. As the summer night sweltered on, John found his mind returning to the pernicious question, his nausea swelling in proportion to his lurid curiosity.

Hours after the rest of his family must have surely been sound asleep, not conscious of the indecency of what he was doing, John left his bed in a near-somnambulant trance. He took his flashlight from the closet and made his way quietly down to the dark mortuary in his pajamas.

The tiled floor was cool under his bare feet.

He quietly slid open the drawer and flicked on the flashlight. Carefully, he lifted the sheet. The garish bruises on Pearl Anne's pretty face startled him. He hadn't been expecting to see that. Most of the serious damage had been done to the back of her head—her skull was caved in back there. This he knew only because he'd read about it in the *Hernville Reporter*.

Then, as if he'd never been taught a lick of respect, John pulled the sheet back further and let the beam of the flashlight travel down the length of Pearl Anne's slender body. She was naked and slightly blue.

John caught his breath. The starkness of her nude skin, its unnatural color, disturbed him. Still, a thought stirred in him: He could never have hoped to glimpse this beautiful body had Pearl Anne still been alive. He steadied the flashlight's beam on her small breasts, her concave belly. Then he swept the light over the thatch of curly dark hair that hid her most secret part.

She was too beautiful, even in death.

John's penis stiffened inside his cotton pajama bottoms. The nausea flooded him again but he couldn't resist his urge to touch her. His trembling fingers trailed lightly over her icy breasts, down her cold, sunken belly, and then lightly across the coarse hairs. Overwhelmed by a sudden passion, John slid his hand inside his pajama bottoms. He hardly needed to touch himself when he came all over his hand.

Safely back in his room a little while later, John waited anxiously for morning, not sleeping a wink, replaying the episode over and over. Sometimes stroking himself compulsively, sometimes succumbing to crippling doubt: Had he remembered to put Pearl Anne's sheet back exactly as he had found it? He couldn't be sure, since it had been dark when he'd slid open the drawer.

Somehow he made it through to morning and forced himself to join his family at the breakfast table. Somehow he managed to sit still as he watched his father head down the stairs to the mortuary to begin his work. Hours later, John himself nervously descended the stairs in time to see his father slipping Pearl Anne into the last of her burial clothes.

"It's such a pity," his father lamented, looking up innocently at John. "She was such a pretty little thing, wasn't she?"

❧

John Skoff Jr. shook himself from his reverie to discover he'd been absently stroking himself as he lay across his parents' old bed.

The night with Pearl Anne's body—normally he resisted allowing himself to remember it. Just thinking of it started a chain reaction of compulsive sexual behavior that repulsed him. The only strategy he'd found for keeping his behavior in check was to keep the memories buried, far from the surface of his brain. But now, triggered by his phone conversation with Camellia, here they were again. His mind drifted over the year that had followed, the ugly, obsessive year, when his grades had suffered. When he almost hadn't graduated and hadn't been able to explain to his parents and his teachers what was going on. So much of that year had been spent indulging in self-abuse, visions of the naked and lifeless Pearl Anne filling his head. How could he have spoken of that?

He remembered his crazy scheme, how it had taken him several months to get up the nerve to ask Camellia out on that date. He'd feared his motives would be transparent, that Camellia would see through him; that she would penetrate his thick fog of filthy thoughts and discover, somehow, that he had fondled her dead sister and was now hungering for a surrogate.

Eventually he'd convinced himself that he was crazy to worry, Camellia couldn't read his mind. He stopped her on the street one day, in broad daylight, and as casually as he could, he asked her out. He couldn't remember now what movie they'd seen, but he remembered he'd taken Camellia to a picture show and had sweated all through the movie, wondering how he would ever convince a girl as young as she was to make out with him in his father's car.

The worst part came when she was easier to seduce than he could have imagined. She hadn't yet learned how to kiss. She exchanged quick pecks with him and never once opened her mouth. But she seemed eager to let his hands explore her. At first it exhilarated him because her face looked just enough like Pearl Anne's to satisfy his obsession. But when she allowed him to unclasp her bra and slip his hand up under it to fondle her small breasts, her breasts were warm and her heart was beating. It unnerved him. It wasn't what he'd expected. Camellia was too vital and too willing. She never once tried to stop his hand from sliding up under her skirt. In fact, she threw her arms around his neck and held him, panting gently in his ear as his fingers found their way inside her panties. But it horrified him to discover the natural heat that radiated out from between her legs. The slippery wetness he felt there was something he'd nearly forgotten girls' bodies did. It was a warmth that asked for something equal in return; a gesture he felt incapable of making.

John's erection shriveled up and disappeared then, and that familiar nausea rolled over him. He was mortified. As calmly as he could, he ended the evening, walking Camellia up to her door and leaving her with a quick peck on the cheek. But for years afterward he made a point of avoiding Camellia's field of vision entirely, so ashamed he was of how his body had adjusted to the dead.

༄

Camellia set a cup of hot black coffee in front of Hank. Then she brought him a small pitcher of milk and a silver teaspoon, a teaspoon that was part of the Johnson family's extensive heir-looms. In this case, a complete set of antique sterling silverware whose two hundred and seventy-six pieces served twenty-four. The Honorable Judge and Mrs. Johnson had stopped entertaining decades ago, however, and Camellia had taken to using pieces of the heirloom silver for everyday use. It was a subtle, almost imperceptible rebellion, but she knew it would have her late, insufferable mother-in-law turning in her grave. It was with a peculiar sense of satisfaction that Camellia now placed the silver teaspoon in front of Hank.

"Do you want to go up and see him?" she asked. "Pay your last respects?"

"No," Hank answered. "Not yet, anyway. I'm more concerned about you, Camellia. Are you handling it okay?"

"Me? I'm fine, Hank. I'm better than I expected. I'm going to get through this, as long as I have you to help me manage things."

"Don't worry," he assured her. "I'm not going anywhere."

Camellia sat down and studied Hank as he sipped his coffee. "Last night," she confided, "after Dr. Elliot left, I lay awake in bed, thinking about the changes coming, and it occurred to me that I'd really like to sell this house, Hank."

He looked at her skeptically.

"I know," she added in defeat. "There isn't a soul in this town who could afford to buy it from me. Maybe I could just redecorate," she decided at last. "Get rid of all this heavy furniture that oppresses me so."

"That's probably the wiser idea," Hank advised, reaching across the table and gently squeezing her hand. "We could have it shipped upstate for auction and you can start over new. It'll be easy enough to do, after the will's been probated."

"Hank, I want to thank you again."

"For what?"

"For telling me about the will. I'm sure you have a good idea of just how much I appreciate it; you're not stupid."

"It's okay. We don't need to discuss it anymore."

"What about Miss Lee? Has she even been told about the will? That it was changed back?"

"Not that I know of, unless Percy said something."

"Was he still seeing her, you think?"

Hank glanced down at his coffee cup, too uncomfortable to look Camellia in the eye. "Yes, I think so. I'm pretty sure he was."

"It's okay," Camellia assured him. "I'm all right with it. I imagine if he was still seeing her, then she hasn't been told anything—if I know Percy and his manipulative way with young women. If Lydia comes forward and tries to make a stink, I'll get through it. It won't be pleasant dealing with, but I'll get through it."

"I know you will."

"I'm so glad it's over, Hank!" Camellia blurted. "I was so sick and tired of fucking that old bag of bones!"

Hank blanched at the intimacy of her remark.

"I mean it," Camellia insisted. "Why an old man like Percy

needed such extravagant stimulation when he couldn't even come anymore is beyond me. But I don't care, I'm just glad it's over. No more sex for me, Hank. I'm done with it. And it's not a moment too soon."

Hank smiled at her with genuine compassion. "But this could be an exciting time for you. You're finally free to play the field."

"What field? I'm sixty-five years old! I'm not interested in playing any field. The only men who'll be interested in me will be after my money, Hank. I'm no more stupid than you are."

"Maybe you're right," he conceded, wondering privately how Camellia might fare as a lover. He'd only considered her as Percy's wife all these years. Now she was a decidedly different commodity. "You never know. Life takes surprising turns sometimes."

When the doorbell chimed again, Hank rose from the kitchen table. "That'll be Skoff's drivers. Why don't you wait here? There's no reason for you to see this."

"It's okay," Camellia said. "Even when that old man was alive he seemed empty and dead to me. The only difference now is that I don't have to take any more of his shit."

⁊❧

Lydia's blond hair was freshly washed and she had on her prettiest flowered dress when she walked into the Hernville County Jail.

Sheriff Palmer was readying to leave his office and head over to Rosie's Diner for lunch.

"Afternoon, Lydia," he said mechanically, but Lydia thought he was looking down his nose at her as usual.

It's okay, she told herself. *Soon enough, he'll discover I'm worth more money than he'll ever hope to make as a measly sheriff. Then he won't be so quick to be haughty with Lydia Lee.*

Dil looked up as Lydia came through the door and could barely conceal his look of chagrin. "Lydia," he called out, his voice catching in his throat and making a hollow, false sound. "What a nice surprise. You fixing to have lunch with me?"

"I sure am," she replied. And as Sheriff Palmer left the station house, she surreptitiously lifted the front of her dress, exposing her perky blond bush to Dil.

"I'm not wearing any panties," she whispered.

"I see that. Lydia, I don't think this is such a good idea. Why don't you go on home?"

"I want to see Cal."

"But we got another prisoner in there now. And I got to stay out here and mind the radio and the phones."

"Who else you got locked in there?"

Dil shrugged uncomfortably. "Peck Baxter, if you must know."

"Peck?" Lydia scoffed incredulously. "That old drunk? He's probably unconscious and you know it. Let me in to see Cal. Come on, Dil, do it. I want to have a few words with that guy. I want to see the look on his dumb-ass face when he hears about all my money."

With a sigh that said this was against his better judgment, Dil got up from his desk and unlocked the door that led to the jail cells. "Don't rile him too much, Lydia," he cautioned her uselessly. "I don't want any trouble."

Lydia passed through the unlocked door without replying. The perfumed scent of her freshly washed hair lingered in Dil's nostrils as he reluctantly returned to his desk, leaving the door ajar behind him.

Lydia entered the cold, sterile room as if she had all the time in the world. Peck Baxter was in the first cell. He wasn't exactly passed out cold, but he wasn't looking like he was feeling too special. Then there was an empty cell between Peck and Cal. Cal was in the third cell down, sitting on his cot.

Just sitting there, thinking about useless shit, Lydia figured.

She pretended not to look his way, but she could feel Cal's eyes burning into her furiously. She stood in front of Peck Baxter's cage, right in his line of vision, so he could get a good look at her. Her dress was already low-cut, but Lydia unbuttoned the top two buttons, pulling the flowered material aside so that Peck could see the rosy pink nipple of her left breast. She winked at Peck and gave him a smile.

"You don't look so good, Peck Baxter," she cooed quietly. "You tie one on last night, did you?"

Peck blinked his eyes and stared hard at Lydia's tit, as if maybe he was wondering if she were only a dream.

"Why don't you haul your fat ass home," Cal spat.

"Why, Calvin. I didn't see you there."

Lydia sauntered over to his cell, keeping her distance from the bars.

"Who you fooling, you bitch? No way you came to see that old boozer."

"You're right, Cal," she conceded, pretending to feel chastised. "I've come to see you, to let you kiss my sweet, fat ass."

"It's fat, all right," he muttered, then added, "Fuck you."

"Not anymore, hot shot. You don't get to fuck Lydia anymore. You only get to kiss Lydia's sweet, fat ass. Well, I take that back: I'll let you lick it, how's that sound? Would you like that, Calvin? Would you like to lick me?"

Cal made no reply, but Lydia could see the muscles in his upper body straining. She knew she'd hit a nerve; only real anger could make Calvin keep his mouth shut.

"Hey, Baxter," she called out, strolling over to Peck Baxter's cell again. "Let me show you something." Lydia turned her back on Peck and lifted her dress up around her waist. "You see the pretty behind I got?"

Peck Baxter sat bolt upright on his cot and stared at Lydia, who was naked from the waist down.

She turned her pretty head around to look Peck in the face. "Calvin over there is addicted to this sweet ass. He just has to have it." Lydia grabbed a sizable portion of her behind. "And I don't just mean he likes to sink his teeth into these cheeks— which he does—what he really likes is to push his nasty black cock into that tiny hole." Lydia turned around completely then, to let Peck Baxter get a good look at her blond bush. "That's what

Cal loves most of all. Even when Lydia says 'No, no, no, Cal; don't stick that nasty black cock into my tiny hole,' Calvin does it anyway because he loves to listen to Lydia scream."

"Why don't you shut up, you stupid slut," Cal called.

Ignoring him, Lydia continued addressing Peck. "Have you ever seen Cal's nasty black cock? Has he ever showed it to you, Baxter? You should have him show it to you sometime. I'll bet you've never seen anything like it, except maybe on a plow horse. He's positively huge."

"I'll show you huge, Lydia," Cal baited her, getting up now from his cot and going to the bars of his cell. "Why don't you come a little closer and get down on your knees so you can get a good look."

"Maybe I will, Cal. Maybe I will."

Lydia strolled over toward Cal again, letting her pretty dress fall back down around her legs, but shoving open the top of it, so that both her breasts were now on display.

"Remember these?" she asked softly as she stood directly in front of him. "Wasn't it you who chewed on them one night until they were purple? If it wasn't you, then it was someone who looked an awful lot like you."

Cal stared hard at Lydia's bared breasts. Then he looked her in the eye. "Come closer and let me kiss you," he told her. "What are you doing here, anyway?"

"I came to tell you the good news." Lydia stepped a little closer to the bars of Calvin's cell.

"What good news?"

"That I'm too rich for you to fuck anymore."

Cal eyed Lydia with complete contempt. "What's that supposed to mean?"

"Judge Johnson died today and I'm a significant inheritor in his will."

"Bullshit, you are."

"I am." Lydia pulled lightly on her nipples, with an eye on the growing bulge in Cal's bright orange overalls, property of Hernville County Jail.

"Why would ol' Judge Johnson want to leave you anything but his week-old trash?"

"Why?" Lydia asked, mockingly. "Did you ask why? I'll tell you why. You see these lips?" Lydia pursed her glistening lips slightly, moving closer to the bars. "Do you remember them? You remember how pretty they looked sliding up and down on you? Well, guess what, Cal. You ain't the only one who thinks these lips look pretty with a cock stuck in between them. And you ain't the only fool who got addicted to my ass, either."

Cal couldn't hide the shock as it slowly registered on his face. "Shit, Lydia, you're serious."

"I'm serious."

"You're gonna be rich?"

"I'm going to be rich. And I wanted to tell you the news in person. I figured I owed your black ass that much. In fact, I wanted to be extra-special nice to you today and let you watch Dil fuck me like a dog right here on this very floor, so you could get a good look at everything you're going to be missing from now on. I was going to let you watch him go into my sloppy pink hole, but Dil is chickenshit. So I came alone."

Cal leaned his face against the bars. "You gonna show it to me anyway?" he wanted to know. "You gonna show me that sloppy pink hole?"

"Maybe. I might bend over and show it to you anyway. I might, because after today, I'm afraid I'm going to be a little too high-class for the likes of you, Cal."

"Is that so?" he whispered, reaching a hand out toward her blond hair. "Bring your face up here and let me kiss you, you bitch."

Lydia let Cal guide her face up close to his and they kissed between the bars, their tongues mashing together while Cal's hands groped Lydia's exposed breasts. When Lydia slid her hand in between the bars and reached for the bulge hidden under Cal's clothing, Cal unzipped his overalls and let his cock spring free.

"Jesus," Peck Baxter exclaimed, his eyes riveted on the display.

Cal groaned when he felt Lydia's hand close around his aching cock. "God," he whispered. "Suck it, Lydia. Come on," he pleaded. "I need to feel your mouth on it, girl."

"Cal, it's too expensive for you now. You can't afford it."

He smiled faintly at her, pushing his dick up into her hand. "Well, what've you got that I can afford?"

Lydia smiled back at him. "You can lick my hole," she answered.

"Make it sloppy?"

"That's right, make it sloppy. Like that night at the Lone Tree Motel, you remember, Cal? You remember that night at the motel?" Her hand continued to stroke the length of his cock.

"I remember."

"What exactly do you remember?"

Cal reached his hand through the bars and slid it up under Lydia's dress. He discovered her snatch was soaking and he slid his fingers into the wet hairs. "I remember bending you over and making you take it like a dog," he said.

"You do?" she moaned in spite of herself, pushing her mound closer to his fingers.

"I do. I remember you down on your elbows too, begging me to shove it up your ass. Begging me, Lydia, because you love to feel my huge black dick filling you up back there."

"You remember all that?"

"I do," he said, finding her slippery clitoris now and rubbing his fingers over it.

Lydia licked her lips. She let go of Cal's cock and held to the bars to steady herself. "Well, I'm impressed," she gasped quietly. "Your memory serves you pretty well. You want to try to fill me up now? Right here?"

"What do you mean?" he asked.

"You want me to bend over right here—"

"So you can press your ass up against the bars?"

"Yes," she panted.

"So you can get your ass fucked? You gotta suck me first, bitch.

I need to be good and wet to fit into that tight hole of yours."

"You want me to suck you?"

"That's right, Lydia," Cal insisted, his fingers rubbing her stiff, swollen clit. "I want you to make me all sloppy wet too. And afterward, you can hold your dress up and bend your white ass over for me. What do you think of that?"

Lydia was overcome with lust. She slid down to her knees and pulled Cal's thick erection through the bars. First she licked the length of him thoroughly; then she lingered over the bulging head, spitting onto the piss slit and pushing the spit around.

Cal moaned deliriously as he watched Lydia's pink tongue go to work on his throbbing black dick. Reaching both hands through the bars, he slid his fingers into her blond hair, keeping it out of her face so he could have an unobstructed view of her mouth. And when Cal had her right where he wanted her— when, with considerable effort, Lydia had managed to fit her mouth around his substantial shaft—Cal grabbed hold of Lydia's neck and jerked her face flush with the bars, his cock finding the back of her tightening throat, his coarse pubic hairs mashing into her nose.

Lydia struggled frantically as the thick cock head cut off her air.

Cal could feel her gag reflex trying to kick in. He saw the tears stream out the corners of her eyes. She punched his thighs, clawed at him through the bars and put up a good fight, but Cal didn't mind. He toyed with the idea of tightening his grip around her neck and watching her eyes bulge, but it was partly the noisy fuss that Baxter kicked up and partly his own desire to get out of jail that made Cal release his hold on Lydia's throat.

She sprang away from him instantly, landing on her ass as she gasped for air. "You son of a bitch," she sputtered, copious amounts of saliva now flooding her mouth and tears still spilling down her face. "You sick pig!"

By now, Dil had heard the commotion and was hurrying toward Lydia, trying to size up the situation.

"*I'm* a pig?" Cal shouted. "*I'm* a pig? You haven't seen anything yet, you cheap piece of shit. Wait until I'm outta here and I get you alone."

"Come on, Lydia," Dil interjected, lifting her up by her arm and urging her toward the door. "Let's get you out of here."

"You're *never* going to get me alone, don't you get it, you asshole? You're never going to touch me again," Lydia screamed.

"I'll touch you, all right," Cal hollered after her. "I don't care how rich you are, I'll touch you in ways you can't even imagine, you white bitch. I might even sell tickets to how I'm going to touch you, Lydia—that's how *I'm* gonna get rich!"

❧

The crab apple trees in Glen Rest Cemetery were in full bloom the morning Judge Percival Whitehead Johnson was laid to his final rest. Camellia was dutifully dressed in black, her perfectly coiffed hair covered by a smart black hat and a simple black veil.

Hank McGwynne stood next to her, his steady arm at her trembling elbow. Hank knew she trembled not from an inability to control her grief but from her fear of intrusions from people she felt she barely knew. Half the town had showed up for the funeral at First Methodist Church and had followed them to the cemetery. Most of them kept a respectful distance from Camellia, but Hank felt protective of her privacy just the same.

Lydia Lee showed up alone. She too was dressed in black, her pretty blond hair pulled into a neat ponytail at the back of her head, adorned with a simple black bow. She stood as near to the burial plot as she could comfortably get, keeping a keen eye on Hank McGwynne the entire time, not even noticing that Camellia was on his arm.

Hank hadn't yet returned any of Lydia's phone calls—and she had made plenty in the three days since Percy had died. She'd only gotten as far as Miss Carver, who was polite but detached and noncommittal about why Mr. McGwynne was proving so hard to reach.

Not one tear was shed as Percy's casket was lowered into the earth. The mourners gathered there were unusually silent. The minister's brief eulogy was punctuated only by a flock of noisy starlings hidden in the blossoms of a nearby crab apple tree, the enthusiasm of the chattering birds at times threatening to drown out the minister entirely. The casket was lowered slowly into the ground. Camellia was on her way back to the car before the first clumps of dirt had a chance to hit the hard surface of Percy's new home.

"Mr. McGwynne, wait." Lydia managed to reach Hank as he was helping Camellia into the black limousine.

Hank braced himself for a verbal skirmish. "Miss Lee." He turned and faced her politely.

Lydia tore into him, oblivious to Camellia's presence in the car, whose door was still open. "I've been trying to reach you for three days now. Haven't you been getting your messages?"

"Yes, Miss Lee, I've been getting my messages. But I'm the executor of Judge Johnson's estate. There's been a lot to do. I'm sure you can understand what my priorities have been."

"But this is *about* Judge Johnson's estate. When are you planning on reading his will?"

"We're going over to the office right now. Why?"

"You know why," Lydia spat.

"I'm sure I don't, Miss Lee. Perhaps you can enlighten me."

"I'm a significant inheritor in his estate and you know that."

Hank closed the car door slightly. He leaned toward her, lowering his voice, his eyes taking in the full depth of her determined expression. "You're under a misconception, Miss Lee. Judge Johnson revised his will nearly a week ago."

Lydia held her ground, unmoved. "What is that supposed to mean, Mr. McGwynne?"

"That there's no provision for you, that's what that means. It was all for nothing, Lydia," Hank told her quietly. "Nothing except the sheer pleasure of getting screwed."

❧

Camellia sat quietly. The voices of Hank and Lydia receded from her attention. She felt sorry for Lydia Lee, coming to the end of it duped and degraded, with nothing to show for her tenacity. Who knew better than Camellia how distasteful intimacy with a nasty old man like Percival Whitehead Johnson could be? Tenacity is what it took to get through even an hour of it. Though it hadn't started out that way. In the beginning, Percy had seemed gallant and almost charming. Camellia could never have been seduced by him had it been otherwise. It was Percy's mother and grandmother who had made Camellia's life so miserable in the beginning, treating her dismissively and rarely approving of a single word she uttered, undermining what little self-esteem she had and always placing her on public display. Camellia had felt that being the wife of the town's only judge was a bit like being a circus freak, only the wardrobe was a lot fancier. Percy's contribution to the torture came later; he ignored Camellia more and more as the years rolled languorously by, days seeming like weeks sometimes and nights seeming like an eternity.

When Camellia and Percy had first gotten married, the sex hadn't been so bad. It certainly wasn't the kind of thrill Camellia had been expecting. But still, the time they spent together making love at night showed Camellia that the busy judge remembered she was alive—even if it only happened once or twice a week. Then, maybe once a month.

It was Percy who'd suggested separate bedrooms after fifteen years of marriage had yielded no children. It wasn't Camellia's body that had betrayed them; it was Percy's. He took it out on her anyway, however, purchasing an expensive home on the other side of town where he would entertain much younger women, sometimes for days at a time. Camellia had found out about the second home soon enough. She suffered the degradation in silence, unwilling to take on the scandal of divorce or surrender even a portion of the affluent life she was now submerged in and accustomed to.

When the day came that Percy threatened to divorce Camellia—of all things!—their rare sexual encounters turned ugly. Barter, bribery—sex became a weapon. It no longer even remotely resembled an expression of conjugal love. From that high-water mark of cruelty, they never looked back. Hatred grew between them, to supplant what had been before. But Camellia dug her trench deep and defended it until the final hour, doing whatever was required of her until victory was won.

She hadn't even pretended to seem bereaved at the viewing. It was only exhaustion that had made her so forlorn.

"Well, I won't be surprised if she shows up at my office, Camellia," Hank said disgustedly as he slid in next to Camellia in the back of the black limousine. "But I did the best I could. It's almost over," he added, taking her hand affectionately.

❧

That night, John Skoff Jr. drew the blinds closed at the front of his house and shut off the lights. He made his way to the kitchen in his pajamas, where, briefly, the light from inside his refrigerator sliced a bright wedge in the darkness. From the top shelf in back, he retrieved his favorite indulgence: a silicone rubber replica of a vagina. It had cost him nearly $200 from a mail order company, but it had been worth every penny. It was pliable and lifelike, and he could keep it quite cold.

He closed the door to his refrigerator, and all was black as pitch again. John made his way down the hallway to the privacy of his parents' old bedroom. Before retiring, he locked the bedroom door—out of habit, for he was quite sure he was alone.

On nights like this, he kept the house as dark as possible. Not from a fear of being observed—it was his strong distaste of catching even the briefest glimpse of himself that drove John into darkness. The cocoon of safety he found there aided his fertile imagination.

He stepped out of his pajama bottoms and got into bed. As John slathered his erection with lubricant, he wondered about that blond who had showed up at the Johnson viewing. That tart from across town, Lydia Lee. He wondered if she was the kind of girl who would be interested in making a little extra money. He pumped his erection vigorously and then wondered if she was the type of woman who could keep her mouth shut.

When he was fully erect, he pushed his slippery penis into the ice-cold rubber vagina, sliding it up and down on himself rhythmically, letting his thoughts wander. First, he created a world in his head where a pretty thing like Lydia would be willing to indulge him: to allow him to fill her vagina with ice, lying perfectly still until it was time for him to mount her. Then he created a world much closer to home, a world where she might die of an unfortunate accident, but nothing too disfiguring. A sudden internal hemorrhage, maybe. Or a freak heart attack, something that would keep her looking pretty but nevertheless dead. Then he could really go to work on her.

Excited, John feared he was going to come too quickly. He slowed his pace with the rubber vagina, taking his time with the' imaginary corpse of Lydia.

ঌ

Camellia checked to ensure the doors of the house were securely locked and the alarm system set before she headed up the stairs to the sanctity of her room. It was over, finally. She was really alone.

Her mind reviewed the events of the last three days. "That godawful viewing," she sighed as she slipped out of her clothes. It had been much worse than the funeral. She'd had to spend six solid hours pretending she appreciated the thoughtful condolences of all the liars in town, who in turn pretended they'd given a shit that the judge was dead.

The only break in the monotony had been when Lydia Lee had shown up fleetingly at Skoff's wearing a too-tight dress with no bra and no discernible underwear on underneath it. Everyone seemed to privately appreciate Lydia's complete lack of taste. "Down to the last man," Camellia said softly, smiling to herself.

Lydia had kept clear of Camellia during her brief trip up to the bier and then back out to the street. But Camellia had watched with interest as Lydia Lee regarded Percy's waxlike figure in the open casket. What was it, Camellia wondered now—a spark of delight? A searing thrill? Something nearly imperceptible had flared in Lydia's face at the sight of Percy's unmistakably dead body. Perhaps no one but Camellia had seen it for what it was— it had been that subtle. But then Camellia herself had fostered a similar excitement upon seeing Percy dead. Perhaps she was the only one in the room who *could* have recognized it.

Poor Miss Lee, Camellia thought to herself. *She came so close to a fortune. But she's still young. She's got a whole lifetime ahead of her and a world full of eager men in which to rebuild her financial future.*

Camellia switched off the light and settled contentedly into her big bed. She couldn't keep her thoughts from straying to John Skoff, how he'd actually gotten an erection while standing right there next to her. It had happened when she'd brought her husband's burial clothes over to the funeral home. One minute they were exchanging meaningless sentiments about Percy. The next minute John had a pained look of embarrassment on his face. It was then that Camellia had noticed John's erection pushing up against his trousers. If he hadn't said, "Excuse me, Camellia," with such heartfelt sincerity, she wouldn't have believed it was happening. Imagine. An erection for her after all these years.

Maybe Hank's right, she mused. *Maybe life still holds some unexpected surprises.*

ও

Across town, Lydia Lee turned out her light and got into bed alone. Now that she was just trash again, broke, with no prospects of inheriting anybody's fortune, she didn't think Dil would even bother to come home. She pulled the blankets around herself and tried to sleep.

Ten blocks away, Cal, fresh out of jail, broke into his uncle's gardening shed. Thinking of Lydia, he quietly rummaged around in the dark for a pair of black utility gloves and some strong, thick rope.

MARILYN JAYE LEWIS is an award-winning erotica writer whose books include *Neptune & Surf,* *When Hearts Collide, In the Secret Hours,* and *When the Night Stood Still.* She has, among many other lovely qualities, a decidedly open mind and a *very* vivid imagination.